About the Author

I am a primary school teacher who loves to read and tell stories to children of all ages. I have my own tutoring business called Achieve with Amy and Friends. I have always written stories for the children I teach and my family, this was a hobby but I always had the dream that one day my books could be published. I believe that everyone deserves to let their imagination flow to create new stories.

To Lena and Orla,
Hope you enjoy
my story
Love
Amy
Watson

The Hooters

Amy Watson

The Hooters

Olympia Publishers
London

First Published in 2022

Olympia Publishers
Tallis House
2 Tallis Street
London
EC4Y 0AB

Printed in Great Britain

Dedication

I dedicate this book to all the children I have taught over my teaching career and to all the families that have worked with 'Achieve with Amy and Friends'.

Acknowledgements

Thank you to my family for believing in me. Thank you to Emily, for being my first reader.

Benjamin Hooter

Tuesday

My mum died on a Tuesday. It wasn't raining. It wasn't sunny. It was a normal day for most people. But not for me. It was the day I had feared for almost two years. We knew it was coming – me and Dad that is. But it didn't hurt any less. Some people say that if someone dies and it's unexpected then it's worse because of the shock. They say that you don't get to say goodbye to the person properly. I think the people that say this clearly haven't watched their mum get sicker and sicker for months and months on end. They haven't spent months sitting there, trying to make someone laugh, but scared that laughter hurts them, when there's so much to say but nothing to say at the same time. They haven't had to walk out of a hospital room terrified that this was the last time, the last goodbye, the last cuddle, the last night. I looked at my mother every day thinking that I didn't want to remember her like this. My mum was strong, funny, incredible, perfect, a superhero and someone who let everybody in. But unfortunately, she also let a disease in, a disease that was going nowhere once it found her. A disease that eventually stole my mum from us. That normal Tuesday night we went from a family to a dad and son – and neither of us knew what to do.

We went back to the house that night in silence. I lived in a small cul-de-sac called Petunia Grove. It was my mum's dream home; she told me how she fell in love with the street even before she viewed the house. She and my dad had driven from the city to the suburbs, in search of finding the perfect family house. They were married just six months when they received grandma's inheritance for a house and had spent many a night talking about their future in their new home – how they wanted it to be a perfect place for their children to safely play outside, how they needed a big overhanging porch to drink tea and laugh together, how important a cosy living room was with a grand fire place and big armchairs that they could grow old together in. It was on their unmapped journey through the suburbs when they wandered into Petunia Grove, and Mum always said it was the second time in her life that she felt love at first sight (my mum was lucky, she said that she actually felt this feeling three times; with Dad, with the house and finally with me). Petunia Grove is (and always has been) a picture-perfect street. Each house is home to a tall blossom tree on either side of the road that tower and fall gracefully over the path with their glittering petals. The houses are grand and important, each with slightly unique features that make them special, but all as equally enchanting and beautiful as each other. Each house has a white wrap-around porch that oozes family life, looking onto large well-kept gardens with perfectly shaped flowerbeds that inject an array of colour into the street. Dad always told the story that when he was driving down the street, he looked over to the passenger side of his old neglected Volvo and saw my mum's eyes sparkle like never before as she watched out of the window in awe of the houses in front of her. He said her smile was undeniable and she had a glow about her that instantly warmed his heart. Dad said that there was nothing he wanted more than to see Mum look that happy for the rest of her life, and so the next day he used the whole inheritance for the corner plot of Petunia Grove.

I often thought about this story while sat in my passenger seat. It would make me smile at the thought being young and in love. But when coming back from the hospital, the thought of this story only brought more tears to my eyes.

We stopped on the drive and both looked up at the house. I knew my dad felt the same as me, but I couldn't quite tell him what that was. He must have been thinking the same as he looked at me and forced a very weak smile onto his face and nodded. It took all of my energy to get out of the car and into the house that I knew was empty. There was eeriness about the house: sadness in the atmosphere. I felt that the house knew what had happened. It was cold and silent. Just like me and Dad. I went upstairs to put on my pyjamas and try and give my dad some space. He was an immensely proud man, and I'm pretty sure he saved his tears for when he was alone. It killed me to see my dad upset and I think he knew that. So being the best Dad in the world even in the worst situations, he stayed strong and tear-free as much as he could when I was around. I tried to do the same for him, but it is a lot harder than you think – after all, I'm only eleven. Maybe I'll get better at it the older I get. I tried to get in bed and go to sleep. But whenever I closed my eyes, I saw the hospital bed that my mum was lay in only two days before and I couldn't bare it. After an hour, I climbed out of bed and gingerly tip-toed down to find my dad.

He was sat in front of the fire, staring into it, mesmerised. His face was wet, but he was silent, his breath couldn't even be heard due to the slight crackling from the logs burning. After what seemed like forever, he noticed me in the corner of the living room and ushered me to come to him. I know that I am eleven and so I should be big enough now to sit on my own, but

13

the only place I wanted to be at that moment was within that cuddle on his knee. He sat me down and his big gorilla arms wrapped me up. He hummed Mum's favourite song slowly, and without realising my eyes began to shut and I finally got some sleep.

Samuel Collins

The Big Move

Petunia Grove, let's face it, it already sounded boring. I knew my mum and dad were acting strange that week. I knew something was up when they let me have ice-cream before my tea one day. I should have seen it coming. They were telling me we were moving. My dad, Dave as I like to call him, has this fancy (but boring) job. He has told me about it, but I have no clue what he does – something on computers. Now he's telling me he has an even fancier new job, but in some new place outside the city. I decided to sit and listen to this crazy idea while they flapped about how to approach it in a positive way. My mum had clearly thought about what to say because it was coming out of her like an award-winning Oscar speech, I decided to put her speech to a halt and really get to the bottom of it.

"So, there's a garden?" I queried, not sure of whether I had heard that right.

"A huge garden, Samuel, you can play football and maybe we could get a tent!" Now to most children, this isn't a big deal – I mean, it's just a piece of grass and a ball. But to me, a boy who had lived in a flat his entire life, and spent most of his Saturdays either walking forever to find a field or kicking a ball against a small wall (and often losing said ball) – this was music to my ears. I have always loved football; watching my favourite players on the television and playing football with my friends in the school playground, but it wasn't *real* football. The space we get is very small and we have to play in between the children who constantly skip and the kids that randomly sit on the floor colouring in – which often meant we got the ball taken from us by the dinner ladies because we accidently get someone with the ball – even though they sit in our way. But I decided to hide this excitement in case I was overlooking what I was really being told here.

"What about my friends?" I gestured to my dad for this question – I could tell my mum was readily prepared for the conversation and already thought of all the answers to all the questions – like mums do. But my dad wasn't so reliable, my dad will slip up and tell me the truth, therefore he was the one I watched for an answer.

"Well…" Dad hesitated, glancing over towards the loving yet apprehensive face on the table that my mother was wearing. The look a mother gives a father when she is trying out telepathy is one of a kind – every mother must do this and so you must know what I'm talking about. It's a kind of I-know-what-you-should-say-so-why-don't-you look. And the replying face of the father is always a mixture of nervousness, regret and trepidation – basically they don't have a clue.

"They can visit! Yes! They can!" My father practically had a golden light bulb shooting out from the top of his head. He must have remembered the rehearsed conversation from an hour earlier and he was proud of it. But then came the word vomit. "I mean, not every day – or every week – I'll be busy I can't be a taxi – but I will be when I can – I will try but what if they are busy – their parents might not like it – we will just have to see – there will be lots of children to make friends with I'm sure though – do you really like these guys so much anyway? I think they're a bit boring – Xbox isn't life after all!"

"Stop, Dave." Quite frankly, Mum had heard enough, and so had I after that Xbox comment.

"Listen." My mum spoke in a delicate tone which did help ease the racketing from good old Dave's answer in my head slightly. "We will keep in touch with your friends here, and we will invite them like we always do, but I am sure you will also make lots of new friends Samuel." She tucked herself under the table slightly and leant closer to me. "Plus, there's a Saturday football team you could join if you wanted to? Everyone there will be your age…" Three points to the mother in the room. She had won. A smile grew on my face instantly and so I nodded my head. The conversation continued, but I forgot to listen as I was too busy picturing the perfect house with the perfect friends in the perfect garden.

This time, my imagination wasn't far off reality. The house was utterly amazing. If I was selling the place this is how I would describe it:

It was a lovely detached house, with a garden all around the house like a moat, which was perfect for a young adventurous boy who liked to lead an exploratory life! The front of the house showcased two of the most perfect blossom trees that stood tall and proud of their appearance. They welcomed spring with an abundance of pearl petals that floated gracefully as if showering the house with glitter in the correct sunlight. At the back of the house, beyond the flowerbed and rockery, and past the patch of grass that would be perfect for a football pitch, was row upon row of tall evergreen trees. They stretched far into the sky and stood tall like an army protecting the house. The house itself was perfect, and a lot different to a city apartment. Its rooms were spacious and hosted their own calming personality, promoting happiness from every nook and cranny. The stairway greeted all visitors, with its long strong arm leading you up to an open landing, mysterious with doors leading lots of ways.

I know. I'm good.

Let's fast forward and two months later, there I was… settled into Petunia Grove. It had taken no time at all to make my room homely, filling the walls with posters of my favourite football players, and showcasing my trophies on the shelf with pride. I had taken to the move like a duck to water, which surprised my parents just as much as me. But the Saturday football team was where I, quite frankly, became a 'legend' and I quickly had a team of friends around me. Life was good.

Mr Hooter

My Wife, Gi

Grief is an unexplainable feeling. I hated myself for being so lucky. Why did I have to go and find the most perfect, incredible, astonishing woman that could ever walk this planet? Why was I lucky enough to receive an undeniable love from this item of perfection? I truly got to experience a one-of-a-kind love, a happiness that is un-measurable. Which is why losing it was so much worse: it was an abomination of despair that hit me like ten thousand bullets all at once.

The day we found out of her illness was a memory I wish could leave my brain forever. A simple test she was having, just to check that all was okay before we started to try for our second baby. When Gi had Benjamin, she really went through a tough time. Her labour was far from perfect, and if anyone else had to endure it I'm sure they would have had everything negative to say if they even got through it, but not my Gi. She never moaned, never grew negative, and never doubted her own ability to successfully deliver our boy. And that's exactly what she did. There was not one moment that went by in the thirty-seven hours where she thought about herself, she was completely and utterly there for the baby – and for me at my times of panic. The midwives couldn't stop commending her, but she merely thanked them for their help to build a perfect family. She doted on us boys completely and I will never ever be able to repay her for the love she shown us. So, when Benjamin grew out of his toddler adventures, we knew it was time to let our family grow. Gi wanted to make sure that her body was ready to support a new life, so we went for simple tests to check she was. I wasn't even going to go with her, she said she was fine, and results didn't come out for two weeks so there was no reason for me to go. But when I woke up that morning, I couldn't bring myself to leave her – just in case. So, we dropped Benjamin off at school and headed for the hospital.

After the initial test, the doctor asked us to wait in the waiting room. She said that there may be further testing needed. Again, with her incredible positivity, Gi agreed to wait and we had a coffee. Gi was saying it was a good thing because we got to have a mini middle-of-the-day date which seemed rare since Benjamin and my new job. We had only recently moved and Gi was adamant we spent our weekends sorting our new house, decorating and making it perfectly ours. And who was I to say no to the beauty that was my wife. But it meant that we seemed to be continually busy for at least a year straight. Now that it was coming together, we were ready to become a four. Gi went into the doctor after about an hour, but it felt like merely a second before she was out again. This time, her smile wasn't so bright. When I asked her, what was wrong she desperately tried to hide some sort of disappointment as she told me we had to wait a little while for a consultant to explain to us. An hour went by while we waited, we watched lots of couples go in and leave straight away. I could tell that Gi was as anxious as I was. We had both fallen silent and sat there, holding each other's hands between the gaps of the uncomfortable waiting room chairs.

"Mrs Hooter?" I remember that voice as if it was my own. The doctor was tall and stern looking, my stomach sank as we both jumped up and walked towards this cold consultant. Was she the bearer of bad news? Is this why she is here? Why she is so cold? Because she has this horrible job of telling couples they aren't ready for another child? If only it was that, if only the problem was that simple. I sat next to my wife in a white room. No posters. No magazines. It was bright white and clean, with a feeling of sadness dripping from the walls. I grabbed my wife's hand as we sat on the itchy sofa. There was no way I was letting go of her; I needed to reassure her because this woman certainly wasn't.

"Unfortunately," she began, which instantly told us the worst was about to be aired, "we have looked at your test results Mrs Hooter. Although some of the results were positive," She paused. Gi had clearly had enough.

"Just tell us. Rip it off like a Band-Aid. We know it's not your fault. Don't worry." There she was, my adorable wife, considering the cold consultant before herself. "We aren't ready to have children? This year? Or are we looking long-term?"

"I'm afraid this is not what I'm telling you." Alarm bells sounded in my head. I thought that what my wife suggested was the worst-case scenario. But here this woman is making out that this could be worse.

"We have found a tumour, Georgina." My brain exploded, my body screamed, every aspect of my life came crashing down around me, but I was unable to move, unable to speak, unable to listen to anything else that the demon sat in front of me was saying. I was frozen still. The white walls of the room were moving in, the atmosphere was blurry, and my brain transfixed on the word tumour like it was in bright lights across my forehead. The sickening feeling was in my stomach. Until I realised, this is not about me, this is my wife and I need to be in the room for her. I need to show her that I am right by her side for this entire journey and we will make it to the other side. I squeezed her hand that now lay lifeless within mine. She looked at me, and slowly raised her hand to my face and wiped away tears from my cheeks. We stared at each other as if we both knew what each other were thinking.

"Do you understand what I'm telling you?" The consultant's voice came back into focus. I think she had been speaking for the whole time, but I wasn't able to process her after her fifth word.

"What is the first step?" I managed to speak, I tried with all my energy to exert confidence and positivity in my voice, and I can only pray that that is the way I sounded.

And that was it. That was – well what I thought would be – the worst memory I would ever have. Because I assumed, things could only get better from here. How wrong I was.

It has been three years since this memory took place, and one week since my wife left us; me and my boy that is. He is the only thing that is keeping me going. I promised to be strong for him; I promised her I would always do right by him. But when you have had the perfect mum in your life, how can I ever give him what she could? We have spent the week in the house, looking at pictures. I can see the sadness in his eyes, the mourning in his heart. Every night we sleep on my armchair because I'm so afraid to be alone. Once he is asleep, I am able to let out my tears, but he often joins me as he cries in his sleep. I don't know what to do. I need her. I need a sign.

Ben

Moving the Furniture

By the second week of my family of three becoming my family of two, we had developed a system to avoid the world. Dad wasn't ready to go out yet and I wasn't ready to leave my dad's sight, so we subconsciously made the decision that we just didn't need to leave the house at all. Dad had quit his job months ago so that he could care for his wife full time. I hadn't been to school either, we had talked about me moving schools so that I didn't have to face everyone's sympathetic faces every day and I could have a fresh start without the tainted memories of the parent sack race that my mum currently held the record for. This didn't bother me as I didn't really have any friends anyway. I think people were scared to talk to me or didn't know what to say to me: either way, I was quite the loner. So, two months ago we took me out of school. That very weekend Mum had a bad turn, we didn't know what was happening but everything that was important on the Friday wasn't by the Saturday. I didn't turn up to the new school I was supposed to, and Dad said that maybe I could sneak sometime in the middle to have off as a family. Now, it seems that we have forgotten about me returning to school altogether – and I liked it that way. I didn't need school – I just needed my dad.

We spent our days looking at old photos of the three of us, our holidays together, our silly summers in the garden, birthdays,

Christmases and anything else we could find. We spent our time both laughing and crying at the time we had as a three, it was soothing and painful at the same time. The nights would be in front of the fire, in the same armchair as the first night we got back from the hospital. I couldn't bring myself to sit in Mum's armchair and secretly I loved being wrapped up in my dad's arms and I think he loved it too. One night, we sat there listening to the crackling of the fireplace and Dad was retelling me the story of the best summer. He explained how Mum would take me to the park every day and push me on the swings for hours and hours and hours; he said that she would not stop because she couldn't bring herself to stop my giggles. But suddenly, he was interrupted by a sharp shriek in the garden.

Now our garden at the back was quite empty. We hadn't done much to it in the recent months, so it was quite overgrown. But at the back of our garden, we didn't have a fence because there are huge rows of trees that run all the way along the street and even further past. Dad always told me that they cut down just over a hundred of these trees to make our road and they weren't allowed to cut anymore so that's why the forest is practically in our garden. When I was little, I remember venturing out and trying to sneak into the forest, but I had only stepped about five strides in and I fell over a big rock and fractured my arm. I had to have a cast for six weeks. Mum always said that it was the worst lesson to learn but at least now we know not to go into the forest. So, after that, I didn't bother with it at all. Sometimes we heard breaks in branches and incredibly early in the morning we always heard a range of bird sounds that we had gotten so used to that we no longer even registered. But this sound was different. It was more exotic than normal, very distinctive and extremely loud. Dad patted my knee and jumped up to get to the window. I followed him, wondering why he was so intrigued.

"Did you hear it?" Dad whispered, as if the something that created the noise would hear us. I don't know why, but I whispered back.

"Yeah, why? What do you think it was?" I stepped forward; I was so close to the window that my breath smeared across the glass. I smiled and went to draw a face in the condensation, but my finger made a sound that I wasn't expecting and it made me laugh.

"Ssshh it might do it again, let's wait!" I hadn't seen Dad this excited for so long. Why was he so intrigued by this creature? Surely it was just a bird? Yet here he was, pulling his old armchair away from the fire and right up to the window. He moved the curtains and set up the perfect viewing spot. It must have been almost midnight, but the moon was full, and the stars were awake. Their light shone down and highlighted the uneven horizon of the huge trees. But the trees were so dark and condensed that they merged together as one.

The shriek repeated. Dad's eyes glared all around the sky, he was longing for something that just wasn't there.

"Dad, it's probably just something in the trees." I tried to speak softly, but I was rather confused by his unexplainable behaviour.

"It's an owl, Benjy" he looked at me with a glint in his eye that warmed my insides, but before I could question this, he interrupted my thoughts.

"Maybe it's too bright in here." I watched my dad run around and switch off all of the lights, considering whether he had finally lost his marbles with all that we have gone through. It was only when he turned to the fire that I grew more suspicious.

"We never turn the fire off!" I announced, now with a clear

annoyance in my tone. Over the last two weeks I had alluded to the fact that the fire was what helped me sleep at night – that and my dad's big comfortable arms.

"But Benjy, we have to." His excitement scared me. I didn't understand. I didn't know if I should try and understand or let him have a small happy moment in this depressed world that we were living in. So, I gave up, and I went to get some blankets for our new spot by the cold window.

Once the house was in complete darkness, we settled in our usual position in the armchair, with the only difference being the view. The forest looked gloomy and frightening to me, but Dad was adamant that we were going to witness something special. An hour passed and there was nothing, my dad's smile was barely there and the glint in his eye was dimming once again. I would never have thought that I would be wishing for an owl, but I really wanted this version of my dad, even if it was just for one night.

"Ben, I'm sorry I have acted so strange." Dad sighed but looked at me for reassurance. "Something is telling me that I need to see whatever is calling us, Ben."

"But, Dad, nothing is calling *us*. It's just a bird. Birds make lots of noises, Dad, we know this." I made a bird noise, a hoot and then a whistle to try and make my dad laugh and come out of this silly trance he was in. But he didn't get my joke. So, I whistled again, but louder.

As I did this, a large dark figure broke the still horizon of the trees; its silhouette grew as the animal grew closer and closer to us from the sky. The body of the beast was round, and it had two outstretched phenomenal wings that made it look like it was floating in the air. I'm certain, that for that space in time, neither myself nor my dad moved even to breathe. The clock struck midnight in the hall and neither of us flinched. The tall majestic figure landed onto the mouldy arm of the porch. The owl was chocolate brown with a glistening white torso. My eyes didn't blink while I scanned every part of it and I noticed that there was a dark black patch on the left side of his chest in the shape of a clean cut diamond; it was exactly where his heart would be. I couldn't help but stare at this beautiful sight in front of me, my mouth was aghast, and I felt completely stricken of any vocabulary. I think Dad was exactly the same, but I couldn't take my eyes away from the window to check. The owl stared dead into my eyes: its mahogany brown eyes made me feel warm and complete. I felt a sense of warmth that I hadn't felt for a long time. I looked at my dad; he had a tear running down his face too.

Mum?

Mr Hooter

My Sign

Another week has gone by and we are still very much surrounded by a deafening sadness. I am trying so hard to be there for Benjamin, but the pain in my heart is excruciating. We are still sleeping in front of the fire, still spending our days looking into the beautiful brown eyes of my wife's photographs, hoping to feel that warmth and tremendous happiness that she gave to us every day but instead to be hit with another stab of unwanted emptiness. I quickly realised that watching television wasn't helping my little one. Everything on it presented us with the ideal family. Every programme contains a mum that is doing right by their child, which only penetrates the knife further into us. I don't want my child to remain in a depressive state. What seems to make him happy is to sit on our armchair in front of the fire and tell him stories about the good old days when me and Gi first fell in love. I see a sparkle in his eyes at the thought of us being happy. It's nice for me I suppose, to remember all of the times when Gi was filled with delight, warmth and at her normal perfect self. I wanted Benjamin to remember his mum this way; I wanted to remember her this way. So, I convinced myself that sharing these stories with him can only be a good thing. I still yearned from something in the universe to guide me. Gi always believed, always promised, that she would be there to show me the light. She told me that, no matter what happened to her, she

28

would be with me until the end of time. I believed her with all my heart, I had to, as I couldn't imagine a life without that being true. But it was now two weeks of not feeling her presence and I began to doubt my own belief. It was not that I hadn't tried. I had sneaked into her dressing room and smelt her perfume; I had read her favourite book. I even spent one day following a ladybird around the house hoping it might spell out something or guide me somewhere where her spirit may be. I was getting desperate and I almost gave up, until that night.

Benjamin had asked me for a story about when he was a baby with Mum, and I immediately searched my brain for my happiest memory I could, until I decided to tell him about the 'summer of giggles' as I liked to call it. I loved watching Benjamin cling to my every word with these stories, and so they often were exaggerated and elongated to help him find sanctuary for longer. I knew that this probably wouldn't go down well with Gi because she always said that true stories are so special because they are honest and so changing a story would be ludicrous. I could imagine her shaking her head but smiling in a cheeky disapproving way. It made me laugh how things like that annoyed her, she was so pure of heart and this was a clear example of that. But this occasion was one of those times where I was going to need to extend the story so that Benjamin had more to listen to, more to enjoy. As the real story ended and the imagination was about to kick into action for my boy an almighty shriek was heard from behind me. It was a deafening screech that stopped me from talking. I stopped. Was this it? Was this the sign I've been waiting for? I instantly darted for the window with all of my hopes flying around my stomach. I don't know what I was searching for, but I knew I had to look. I barely noticed Benjamin as he joined me at the window. I ignored his confused sighs as he pretended to be interested in my thoughts. There was something in my gut guiding me, this was what I needed, and I wasn't about to drop it any time soon.

There it was again! It sounded like an owl, but I knew that there was more to it than that.

A fire ignited in me and ran through my veins. I felt warmth that I thought no longer existed inside me. This was it. She was calling me. She was here and ready to help me through it and save my boy. Why I ever doubted her I do not know. Soon, she will show herself in whatever form that may be, and we will be complete again. We will be a three. I will be able to move, leave the house even. With her beside me, I can do anything. I knew that Benjamin was watching me with glaring eyes. I can imagine that this was strange to him, as he doesn't know what I know. He doesn't know what she promised. But he soon will — as soon as it happens. Then he can join me in this happiness and he too can see the light from this dark dark tunnel that these past few weeks has been. I waited, nose against glass waiting for that calling again. Time seemed to start to slow down while waiting and I saw that Benjamin was growing more and more confused. I tried to get him excited, without making him think that I had lost my mind. I moved our chair closer to the window and turned off the whole house.

It wasn't until thirty minutes later that a fear hit me that I had missed my guidance. I had longed for a sign every second of the day for weeks now, and then I miss it. Benjamin thought I was crazy. I can see it in his eyes. But he gets his politeness from his mother and I know he would go along with whatever I say in order to be polite and keep me happy. His best traits are from his mother. He is going to grow into a hell of a man one day, thanks to her. It breaks my heart to know that she won't be able to see what he becomes; she won't witness him falling in love the way we did. What if I ruin him? What if I undo all the good that she has done in his first ten years of his life? How can I be trusted with the responsibility of his morals, his understanding of the world, his life?

It was now more than ever that I needed to know that there would be guidance from her. I needed to know that she will be with me to correct my mistakes and to fix my wrongdoings. I am nobody without her and I know that. Benjamin probably knows that too. I looked at the small version of her that was sat on my lap. He needed me to be strong. He didn't need me to be this crazy person who is looking for what could potentially just be an animal for hours on end. I needed to give up on this hype and face reality. But first, I needed to explain to my boy.

"Ben, I'm sorry I have acted so strange." I looked at my boy's confused face who clearly agreed with my last statement. "Something is telling me that I need to see whatever is calling us Ben," I watched his face change. All of a sudden, I felt my son grow up. I felt his body stiffen as if he was about to deliver bad news. Was he becoming the adult here? He raised himself up onto the arm of the chair, as if to show that he was taking control of the situation. I had never seen him like this. I had never seen him be mature in a way that made me feel smaller. He began to speak, and I held onto his every word.

"But, Dad, nothing is calling us." He emphasised the 'us' and I appreciated that. We are a team, however small, however crazy, we are still a team. I loved this boy more than he would ever understand. He continued, "It's just a bird. Birds make lots of noises, Dad, we know this." I couldn't help but show my emotion. He was staring at me, looking for an ounce of understanding from his dad and here I was acting disappointed when he told me the vicious truth. I knew he had felt my disheartened feeling when he started making silly noises to make me laugh. Something his mum taught him for sad times, and on this occasion, he nailed it with his bird noises. I smiled and thought about how proud I am of my Benjamin. But he jumped and pointed to the window. That's when I saw it.

Everything that I had been looking for appeared before me. My love was flying towards me like a superhero coming in to save the day – to save our day. I barely noticed the clock in the hall strike midnight as the magnificent creature landed in front of our eyes. I didn't know what to expect in this 'sign' that I was hoping for, for so long. But this beat every expectation that I could have ever of had. I stared. Benjamin stared. Perfection in true form had appeared to us on our porch. The owl stared down, and I noticed its beautiful brown eyes. They were entrancing. They were the eyes of my wife.

Tears escaped me and Benjamin noticed, but at this point I didn't care. I knew he was feeling exactly what I felt. I needed to remember exactly what had happened to entice her to us, the whistling, the clock, the unforgiving smile from my boy. Seeing her was all I needed to fill my heart with content. The bird watched us fall asleep together with smiles on our faces.

The next day we spent the day talking about the miracle that was the night before. We kept our armchair in front of the window and waited for midnight. Benjamin giggled as he whistled his whistle and again, we were lost for words as our happiness arrived in the form of an owl. After a week of staying up late to see my wife and falling asleep in her presence, I decided that enough was enough. I didn't want to be tired when she was around. I wanted to be wide awake and enjoy her for longer. So, I spoke to Benjamin about rearranging our lifestyle.

We didn't need to leave the house, so often we didn't know what to do in the day times other than wait for the night to come. If we were to follow the nocturnal nature that owls have, we could spend more time with my darling and we could sleep during the day. Benjamin instantly agreed with me. He seemed to be happy with anything I said now. So soon enough me and my boy separated from reality all together. We blacked out our windows and day became night while night became day.

Samuel Collins

Neighbours

So Petunia Grove turned out to not be boring after all. I could play all the football I wanted because my friends all lived on the street. Sometimes we would go bike-riding too. I now don't understand why children chose to be inside when they could be outside. And I hate to admit it, but Dave was right about the Xbox. The summer was definitely my favourite time of year, the sun allowed me to get away with staying out for longer each school night and the weekends meant that we (me and my friends) could pitch up a tent at one of our houses and sleep under the stars. It was a tight-knit community in Petunia Grove. Everyone knew everyone; you couldn't walk down the street without expecting a hello from every person or house porch that you passed. But with that came the living CCTV of the neighbours – we couldn't really do anything because of the number of eyes that were around wherever we were on the estate.

Petunia Grove was home to a breadth of families, all different shapes and sizes but all very lovely. There was: the Burgundys; an elderly couple who spent their time sitting on their blue wrapping porch at the top of the street (door number 1 and proud of it!), The Foy family: who where a heart-warming welcoming young couple who had moved in three years ago with a young boy called Jay (one of my friends), The Daniels: these were a career-driven couple who married but went down the cat route for a family as they were barely seen at a reasonable hour due to their demanding jobs, next was the Wilson-Byrne family; a hopeless romantic gay couple who have an adopted son called Noah (another of my friends) and finally the Kettlenot Family: the Kettlenots had two sons – Gordan and Graeme – who were non-identical twins. This was a fact that no one believed as the twins looked like a mirror image of each other. The only difference being a tiny birthmark at the back of Graeme's head, which was often covered by his curly knotty hair – much like his brothers. They too were part of my tribe and in my football team.

There is one other house on the street, this house was simply ignored and quite often forgotten. It fit in with the rest, it surprisingly didn't look derelict, and it was clean and well-kept, much like every other house on the street. Yet no one lived there. Over time there had been many stories of where the owners where. Some said that they won the lottery and they left that very same day without thought to selling the house. Other rumours were that they all caught a disease and died together in hospital, and because the house went to the little boy who had also died, no one realised, and the house remained alone. Yet the house had remained well-kept. There were no signs of paint stripping on the porch, there were no broken windows, there was no leaves gathering or even dust settling on the windows.

The families on the road often spoke about what to do about the house, should they report it or look into it? But as much as this conversation arose it ended just as quick due to the fact that they were all scared of what might happen if someone did move in. Would the ambience be ruined by the newcomers? Would the happy, drama-free atmosphere come crumbling down around them? And so, they decided, as a whole, that the house was none of their business. Anyway, it wasn't as if it was an eyesore on this picture-perfect cul-de-sac because it looked just as good as the rest. There was no negative to it being empty as far as the residents were concerned.

But me and the boys on the street often rode past on our bikes wondering about the mysteriousness of the old house. For so long we had talked about breaking in and finally seeing what was hidden behind the curtains. But we never dared to do it. Last Halloween though, we were close. We had planned a break-in during the 'trick or treat' part of the evening. I mean, we were thirteen now, and the novelty of trick or treating had worn down, especially against the idea of an adventure into the haunted house (it had never been known as this, but since it was Halloween it seemed to make sense). We realised that during that time there was a lot of strangers roaming gleefully around the streets and so no one would take notice if someone was at the empty house. It was obvious that these strangers wouldn't know of its derelict nature so they may very well walk up that path and knock on the mahogany door expecting a lollipop or two. With the watching Burgundys on the other side of the house, this was the only way they felt that I (and the boys) could get to the house undetected. The Burgundys did have a constant watchful eye over the neighbourhood. So, we had it planned, we would simply try the old door, if not the windows, surely there was a way in somewhere. The twins were the bravest of the gang (probably because there were two of them) and so they had offered to go first.

As the evening approached and the darkness grew, the freshly prepared pumpkin lights lit up all doors in the street bar one. Again, this neighbourhood looked like an almost picture-perfect street (I'm actually surprised that one of the neighbours didn't go and put up a pumpkin on the empty house, just to show synchronicity with every house). Slowly, we walked up the path to the house (twin first of course) I had to pretend that I was confident and not worried at all at this point, even though that wasn't what my insides were telling me. I don't know why, but I glanced up to one of the bedroom windows of the building we were approaching. Surely, my mind was playing tricks on me. I instantly rejected the thought that I saw anything. It *had* to be my mind playing tricks on me. I dipped my hand under my monster mask and rubbed my eyes, before glancing up again. There it was. The curtain was open. Only an inch or two, but it was more than I had ever seen before. I didn't know what to do so I nudged Jay. I needed a second opinion.

"What?" Jay grunted, clearly, he wasn't the most relaxed person on this night either. I didn't speak but merely looked at Jay and then moved my eyes in the direction of the window anticipating a shock from my friend.

"What?" Jay repeated, now clearly annoyed that he had lost focus of the task ahead. I looked up to the window again, was Jay that stupid that he couldn't play spot the difference with a house he sees every day of his life? But no. The curtain was closed and unmoved. The house remained still. I stopped dead.

"But…" I couldn't understand. Was I going mad? Had the Halloween night got too much for me? Was this my imagination again? The boys noticed that they had lost some warmth from the tight-knit slow-motion huddle that was once moving as one down the path and turned to face me, stood alone.

"Scared Samuel?" Graeme taunted.

"Want to play trick or treat instead, Baby Sam?" Noah giggled. Noah didn't normally speak up in situations like this; he tended to be the sensitive one. So, this seemed to shock even him. "Sorry," he whispered, regretting his decision to join in. This was soon forgotten as the boys were presented with a very frightened Gordan jumping in between them all.

"What's up with you now!?" Graeme seemed almost embarrassed by his brother's odd behaviour. But Gordan didn't speak. He simply raised his right arm and pointed his finger towards a bedroom window. The curtain was open. Not open by an inch like I had originally seen. But open. Fully open. There was a deafening silence as we all turned to face each other, seeing the petrified faces of my friends confirmed somehow in a mutual decision and so we all instinctively sprinted back to our own houses locking the door behind us. Halloween was over. I fell asleep that night with my mind blown about what was inside the house: a million questions, all unanswered.

There was only one thing for it, we needed to go back.

Mr Hooter

Nosey Neighbours

It had been almost two years of living our lives the way we did. My boy and I hadn't seen another human for a while now, other than our shopping delivery guy who didn't question why we picked a 4am delivery slot because his eyes were barely open enough to see us in the first place. But that's how we liked it. The neighbours weren't an issue because during the years that Gi was alive but sick, we tended to be out of the house most of the time anyway. Lots of the neighbours now are new too, as far as I'm aware. The only voice I do recognise from time to time in the street is old Burgundy's. He has been here since the houses were built and I can't imagine he has even left that rickety rocking chair on his porch. He is the only one I worry about as Gi often made the Burgundys muffins or cookies back when she was well. She would always tell me that it's essential to show kindness to your neighbours, as they might need us, or we might need them down the line. But once she became ill, her world became me and Benjamin up until she needed to be in hospital full time. So, I guess that the Burgundys backed off to give us some space. Maybe they think we left when Gi left. I didn't think that they had ever seen us – but I may have been wrong.

The system we had now was that we would get up about 11pm to get ready for our nightly visit from Gi. She always arrives, as astonishing as ever, at midnight – she always did like routine – and now we have been able to get her to come inside the house and sit with us. We feed her as she perches on the arm of her old chair by the fire. The feeling when she is near is unexplainable; the look my boy gives that bird is true hope and happiness. We don't even need to talk when she's there. Benjamin seemed to be as happy as I am. Deep down I knew that there is a feeling of guilt. I knew that this life isn't a normal life for my boy. He hadn't stepped foot in a school in years, and although I always make him read aloud to me and Gi, and he speaks as though he's lived on the earth for sixty years, I probably am not giving him the education he deserves. But as much as I have these feelings, I also can't help but live in the moment with my dear wife. I can't pull my son away from his mother again; he needs her, and love is more important than education. So I keep these guilty feelings deep down in the pit of my stomach, and I force them to stay there so that I can avoid taking any action on them and so I can stay in the present, in my family unit, just the three of us.

I had avoided these feelings for a good few weeks until the night of Halloween. I knew that our sleep would be tricky on Halloween because there's so much going on in the street and although we tended to not get many disturbances at our door these days – Halloween was a definite reminder that normal people don't sleep in the daytime. So the morning came and me and my boy had said our heart-wrenching goodbyes (they never got any easier even though we knew it was only for a few hours), watched Gi fly off magnificently back into the trees and we were getting ready for bed. I had suggested to Benjamin that we should sleep upstairs that day so we could get a better day's sleep. But I had the ache in my stomach that I knew as guilt and I couldn't sleep. Halloween is a holiday that all children should enjoy. It

40

was another aspect that I had taken away from my boy. I knew he wouldn't change seeing his mum every night for the world. I knew that given the choice; he would want to live as we do. But that didn't make it right. I brushed his overgrown hair away from his eyes with my fingers as I watched him sleep. He no longer cried in his sleep, and as I stared at him it was almost like he was smiling back at me. I loved him so much it hurt. I wanted to do right by him, but I couldn't do it without Gi, and I knew that. Being awake in the daytime was odd for me now. I listened to the people outside living their normal lives; giving kisses at the door as they said goodbye to their spouses and drove off to work, reading the morning paper on the porches with a hot cup of tea, children moaning that they didn't want to go to school and then a few hours of quiet with the occasional runner passing by or dog walker strolling passed talking to their dog like it was human. Then again, who am I to say it wasn't – I'm madly besotted with an owl. I must have fell asleep for the return of the people into their houses after a day at work or school because it wasn't until I heard my own doorbell ring that I awoke. I lay still, careful not to wake up my boy beside me. I didn't want him to wake and listen to the happy children who now wore a range of frightening yet hilarious costumes as they laughed and took photos of their friends in between knocking on doors of strangers and expecting gifts. I didn't want my boy to feel like he was missing out. I listened for the footsteps to get quieter, knowing that the children had moved on before I decided to get up. I tip-toed as quietly as I could to the bedroom window and opened the curtain by an inch. The world outside was different and peculiar. It wasn't exactly daytime, as the sun was setting, but it was the brightest that I have seen the place in a long time. It was an unnerving feeling to watch the children having a good time outside, but I couldn't seem to peel my eyes away. Was this what my boy would look like if the universe wasn't as cruel as it was for taking his mother from him? Would he be out there laughing with people his own age? Socialising with multiple humans is not something my son has done in years. Am I doing right by him? This was the question that felt engraved into my mind and my heart, yet the answer was nowhere to be seen.

My anxiety-ridden trance ended as fear alerted me. There was a group of boys walking up the path of my house. I stepped back from the window, terrified and unable to breathe. No one could know we were here. As I stepped, a floorboard creaked and I noticed a boy at the back glance up at me and then back to the door. Without thinking, I shut the curtain back over as soon as I could. I heard the boys begin to talk. My world spun as I realised that if this youngster did see the curtain open, and now its shut, he will know I'm here because it's moved. So again, I did the wrong thing. I opened the curtain. I couldn't remember how far it was open originally, so I took a guess. As I hid behind the curtain the silence was deafening. I was certain that now they definitely knew that I was here. The epiphany of footsteps that preceded the silence confirmed it.

What was going to happen now?

Ben

People

My new life was normal now and I loved every part of it. I felt like going to bed in the morning and getting up in the night was a special adventure, a secret that only me, my dad and this new version of my mum knew about. I was willing to do anything to make sure that it never changed. I didn't care that I hadn't seen the sun in forever, I didn't care that I had no friends, I didn't care that my clothes were small, or that I hadn't been to school. My dad knew everything I needed to know anyway. He taught me how to fix things in the house and we spent loads of time reading. I was genuinely happy. It wasn't until winter announced itself that I felt like my dad was changing slightly. The eternal happiness that I witnessed in his eyes whenever Mum was around had faded slightly and it was almost as if there was worry in his voice. He hadn't been sleeping as much and so he seemed more tired than usual. Dad had become obsessed with the windows, making sure the curtains were completely shut and checking them multiple times through the night – and I'm pretty sure he did it in the day when he was meant to be sleeping. He now spoke in whispers at all times and he didn't want to go out and get Mum anymore. I did it, and I was happy to, but he watched me from behind the curtain as if there was a bear about to pounce on me. I didn't understand what had gotten into him. We had lived like this for years now and never been seen, spotted or spoken about.

So why all of a sudden was he worried about neighbours? It was the middle of November when I decided to ask him, as two weeks had been long enough for this mood to blow over, and it hadn't.

"Are you okay, Dad?" I asked this in a way that I tried to be nonchalant, but I think it came out the opposite. He looked at me with the same warmth in the corners of his smile that he always has when he is trying to reassure me.

"Yes, Benjy. Are you?" The second two words had a different tone; it was as if his worries hung in the balance of the answer. Why would Dad be worried about me? I was the happiest I had ever been, he is providing me with the best life. Why on earth would he think that I'm not okay?

"Of course, I am. I'm great I'm—"

"Benjy." My dad interrupted me in a way that I dreaded the rest of his sentence. "Do you ever wish things were different?"

"Nope. Not in any way." I announced this with conviction and determination. It was one thing that I was absolutely sure of and I wasn't about to play it down. That seemed to end the conversation as he smiled with hope in his eyes. I loved my dad more than anything. I couldn't imagine living life any other way.

"If someone sees us, Benjamin. We could be in trouble."

"No one has seen us though, Dad, you're getting paranoid. We are safe; we have mastered the art of our life now. It will never change." Dad looked at me like he needed to tell me something. The worry in his expressions flowed out of him. It turned my stomach to think what he was about to tell me.

"Benjamin. There are boys in the street who are getting to a mischievous age; they are about your age. I think this place intrigues them. I'm afraid it is going to get the better of them."

My mind was flooded with questions. I hadn't really thought about the people in the street, let alone them being my age. Would they have been my friends? Who are they? Why would they be interested in my house? How will we stay safe? No matter how many questions I had about these strangers, the feeling of protecting our wonderful night-time life overruled.

"Ok, Dad. What do we need to do?"

Samuel Collins

Moving Curtains

As a week went by, each of my boys' stories became more and more extravagant. Gordan claimed he had seen a six-foot-four man of pure muscle standing in the window using his huge right hand in a clenched fist punching the flat palm of his left (equally large) hand in slow motion and staring at the boys. Noah insisted that there was no man, but that there was a white light of a ghost, hovering above the ground ushering the boys to come in. I came up with many stories, like I always did with my imagination, until I didn't even know which one I believed. But the same outcome was had by all of our families. No one believed us. Eventually, we grew annoyed that they weren't being heard and decided that the house needed further investigation.

The winter was now limiting our time together. The sun went missing almost within the hour of us getting out after school, which we hated as our time to come in depended on when it got dark. This made it hard for us all to plot up ideas to get back to the house. They tried to run past and get looks here and there, but it was impossible. The Burgundys, although old, still remained in their rocking chairs on the porch, with a full visual of their beloved street. There was no way of walking up to the abandoned house unseen. Gordan and Graeme pretended to kick the ball too far once and got up the path, but it was very quickly followed by old Mr Burgundy checking in and how they were 'down the other end' – as if four houses down was another country. It seemed that Mr Burgundy looked for any opportunity for a chat, maybe it was because he was old, maybe it was because they didn't get many visitors often, but either way trying to sneak into the house didn't seem like an option and so we were stuck with what to do.

Saturday opened its eyes and we were all out early. This was a full day that we could stay and explore. Frost had grown on the cars overnight like an unwanted yet blissfully sparkly weed spreading across the street. The air was misty; it showcased our breath and hurt our cheeks and earlobes. But that wasn't going to make us go inside. We wrapped up in layers and layers from head to toe: double socks, wellies that were too big for us, football skins under our trousers and god knows how many jumpers beneath our ski-like coats. All of us wore hats, scarves and gloves. Not only was there barely any skin visible, but we struggled to hear each other through the wool around both our itchy mouths and our numb ears. But we had to allow this amount of clothing as it was the only reason that we were allowed to be outside. Each mother took the approach of *'you have to wear whatever Noah has to wear'*. This did make sense as Noah **hated** the cold. I mean he ***hated*** it. We would all joke that they think Noah would give up Christmas if it meant there was never a cold day. I could see that Noah did consider it but laughed along with the joke and pretended that he didn't agree. So, Noah was more than happy to grow an extra metre in width if it helped him feel warm underneath it all – therefore the rest of us had to unfortunately follow suit.

The wintery attire meant that we couldn't really run to play football and we even struggled on our bikes – the icy tarmac on the paths didn't help either. So, we had to settle for walking, kicking a ball and hatching ideas around the unknown house. All of a sudden, black ice made Jay the victim of a mighty fall. He screamed, ran on the ice before suddenly in what seemed like a slow-motion summersault and then a very heavy land onto his back with the loudest thud you could imagine! He was quickly followed by the twins, who had creased over onto the floor in fits of giggles. I instantly turned as I noticed the Daniels at their window, checking what was going on. I then looked over to the old Burgundy's, who had also stood up and were leaning over their porch. Not a second later, my mum was shouting from the front door to check if everyone was okay. Next, I glanced at the abandoned house where I saw the living room curtains edge open and shadows appear. There was someone in the house! Instantly, without helping my fallen friends I edged over the road to get a closer look. I tried to make it look like I was going back to my own home, so I didn't scare the shadows away, to where my mum stood anxiously at the door, but my eyes were in a trance at the window and I couldn't help but stare. Who was it? I had to see. But I had no luck. By the time I reached the kerb the house had returned to its natural empty self, with closed curtains and an eerie atmosphere. Deflated, I turned back to my friends, ignoring my very confused mother at the door in the process. The boys were up now, but Jay was re-enacting his gold medal worthy fall in a comedic fashion while the others jeered him on.

"Did you see?" I whispered, ignoring the current conversation that was mid-flow, because clearly mine was more important.

"Of course we seen, he went flying!" announced Graeme, wiping a humour tear from his eye before it froze onto his face.

"No. Everyone came to look…" I tried to gesture towards the whole street, hoping to get them to catch onto what I meant.

Noah looked at the boys and then at me as if he was baffled

by my odd behaviour.

"Yeah, Sam. He screamed like a girl for about thirty seconds! I bet everyone heard him!" Noah was chuckling now even though he had been punched in the arm by Jay for calling him a girl.

"No," I attempted to explain again "E-v-e-r-y-o-n-e looked. As in everyone. Everyone on the street. Every. Single. House." I looked around the circle that we were now subconsciously huddled in. I could tell by the looks on their faces that Noah and Jay had twigged – finally.

"What?" Noah said and spun his head quickly round to the direction of the house in question. "What?" He repeated in disbelief.

Graeme and Gordan were now moving their eyes from me to Noah and back. It was if they were watching a tennis match, yet they still had no clue what the boys and I were talking about and their faces were dumbfounded.

"The curtain moved downstairs, and I saw shadows." There was a flare of excitement in my voice now.

"Shadow- ssss?" Jay replied, emphasising the fact that I had used a plural word.

"I think so." I nodded.

"Nonsense!" Gordan jumped out of the huddle as he realised what was actually going on. So, we decided to walk around the street in laps and discuss what had happened. I was not altering my story this time in case I forgot the real parts. But we could not see anything each time they passed the same house.

"Maybe that's it. Maybe that's our plan. Let's do something that makes everyone need to come to their windows. Then we can set up and see if *everyone* does." I announced, hoping that this was finally the plan that we needed and so desperately seeking agreement from everyone in the conversation.

"I'm not falling over again, mate. I know I'm solid but I'm pretty sure I'm as bruised as a peach!" Jay had pain in his voice when he confessed this.

"We need something bigger than you falling over Jay." Noah added, seriously considering how this could work. I was glad that they were on board and felt like finally we were getting somewhere.

Ben

People

My dad wasn't wrong about the boys in the street. Strange things started happening and it became so difficult to stay asleep through the day anymore. It all started when one of the boys screamed louder than I have ever heard. Me and Dad instantly jumped up out of bed and dashed down to the living room thinking something terrible had happened. It was so loud it could have been from inside our house. When we looked through our slither of curtain it was just the friends laughing at each other in what seemed like a pile on of humans. But just as we let the panic lose our thoughts one of the boys seemed to be walking over to our house. Instinctively, we both retreated from the window as carefully and silently as we could. Dad putting one finger to his lips and glared at me with profoundly serious eyes, but I could still see him, the boy. It was strange to see someone a similar age to me, he was wearing loads of layers, but his curly blonde hair flicked over his bobble hat and although he was quite tall, I think he was younger than me. But eventually he turned his back and returned to his friends.

In the days after that we were awoken almost every day. Strange noises, loud music, and one time it even sounded like an explosion. Dad said that the boys must be trying to lure us out. He was again convinced that they had seen us, and he spent most nights trying to soundproof the world from our house – instead of spending time with me and Mum. He was a man on a mission, and he made me promise to never go to the windows, no matter what we heard outside. I think he could have had a point about the boys, but that he had also taken this too far, I bet they were just playing or doing mischievous things that the boys in my books do. I bet they had no interest in us at all anymore and it was all paranoia on my dad's side. But I wasn't about to tell him that any time soon, so I let him do whatever he needed to make himself feel better. And I stayed away from the windows. It soon quietened down, and we began to sleep through the whole day again. This may be because the boys stopped, or maybe my dad's home-made sound proofing actually worked. But either way, I was glad that our abnormal life became normal again.

Samuel Collins

Camping Season

Spring has finally sprung meaning that my back garden is dry enough for a tent. Because we normally don't camp so early in the year, it took a lot of persuading to get my mum on board – but I finally got there. It seems like it has been the longest winter, so setting up the tent with the twins left me with a feeling of relief and excitement. We preferred it to be in my back garden because I had the 'empty' house next to me so there was less chance of any neighbour complaints if we stayed up late. After the boys brought their sleeping bags round and we sorted our snacking situation – which seemed to be the biggest priority – we sat around the lamp pretending it was a fire. Graeme and Gordan had a competition about who could tell the scariest story and Jay continued to try and beat his record of how many marshmallows he could fit in his mouth at once. That was until my mum ruined the fun by coming out of the back door to tell us to get in our sleeping bags or everyone was going home. I knew that as soon as we lay down we would lose Noah, he was a sucker for a sleep and could literally fall asleep mid-sentence if he was lying down.

Then it wasn't long before I found myself lying alone, with a bunch of heavy breathers all around me. I lay on my back, slightly annoyed at my friends for falling asleep on our first camping night, continually throwing a tennis ball to the ceiling of the tent and catching it with the same hand. The air was getting colder so I knew it must be getting late. Out of nowhere, a screech deafened my ears and I jumped out of my skin. I looked around at the boys, but they didn't budge, how did that not wake them up? It was as if there was an eagle sat on the tent it was that loud. I sat up, and the noise sounded again. That wasn't a normal Petunia Grove noise; I would go as far as to say it was more likely Jurassic Park. As I listened intently, trying not to breathe so I could hear this creature, I did not expect to hear a door bang. I figured that my mum had heard it to and come out to check on us, at least I wasn't going crazy and I did actually hear the noise. So, I unzipped the internal and external doors of the tent and popped out my head to reassure my mum that a pterodactyl hadn't taken me. But she wasn't there.

I looked towards the twins' house, but there was no sign of a worried Mr and Mrs Kettlenot either. I wondered whether they were in the garden rather than on the porch, which is why I couldn't see them, so I wandered out of the tent towards the fence to pop my head over. When suddenly, another door banged, and I realised I was at the wrong fence. The hairs on my neck rose and I froze on the spot. Was it the empty house? I tried to slowly turn, without letting the crisp grass crunch beneath my feet. But my excitement got the better of me and my eyes were already fixed on the mysterious house that I had lived next to for so long.

There was nothing. No movement. No sound. Nothing.

I sat on the grass that was now damp and stared at the house some more, trying to revisit everything that had happened. A screech. No two screeches. A door. I went to the twins' fence. Another door. I'm a dope.

Of course, the person or alien or whatever it is that came out of the door the first time, must have gone back in. But what on earth was the screech? Why so late?

It felt like an hour had passed before the cold had turned to freezing and I decided to retreat back into the tent to the not-so-blissful noises that my sleeping friends expressed. That was my chance again and I had missed it. I couldn't wait to tell the boys, and I already knew I wouldn't let it slip past me again.

I didn't realise I had drifted off until the Noah shouted wake up down my ear and gave me the fright of my life. Being the one to fall asleep first, he was also the one who tended to get bored quickly when he woke up on his own, so although I should be used to this because it happens so often– it still scared the living daylights out of me. If that wasn't enough, the twins then launched themselves over the top of me to get to Noah, until we were all in a heap of humans laughing our heads off.

"It was cold last night, I barely slept. Maybe it's too soon to camp." Noah said this, and I instantly knew he was lying because I was up all night and he definitely wasn't—

"Last night!" I jumped up and hit my head on the top of the tent. The boys giggled and didn't take any notice on my sudden excitement.

"I saw the neighbours!"

"Us?" Graeme suggested, as if I was really that stupid.

"The other side, doofus!" I hit his forehead, showcasing where his stupidity was coming from – as if there was a brain in there anyway!

"Oh, not again, Sam. You say this and it's always conveniently when we aren't there or are asleep. Did you dream about them again?" Jay wasn't impressed. It didn't look like the others were either. They had long grown tired of my fascination after we had a million different failed attempts at spotting them in the winter. But I was telling the truth and it was so infuriating. So, despite their uninterested faces, I told them all about my evening; how they fell asleep and missed it, how I was out of the tent and everything.

"So." Noah looked as if he was taking it in. "But." Okay his attitude was changing. "You didn't actually see anyone?"

"No," I confessed. "But it was definitely that side." I was adamant about this, no dreaming, and no imagination. Not this time.

"It was probably just old man Burgundy taking a porch patrol like he does in the day. Bet he does it all through the night too." Jay was confident with this, and he looked proud of himself for thinking of it so quick.

"Fine." I announced irritated that I couldn't convince them. "You watch. I'll show you. Tonight."

The boys laughed at what they thought was my crazy mind off on one again, but they still agreed to camp another night so that they could witness what I saw. In my head I knew I had no idea if it would ever happen again, but I had to try something to prove it to them.

Mr Hooter

The Routine

My paranoia of the neighbours had finally settled, and I had gone back to enjoying my life with my boy. He was maturing and growing so gracefully, and I was so proud of him. I was always told that the teenage years were the hardest. Me and Gi often sat up and talked about the kind of teenager he would grow up to be, but I don't think either of us dreamt he would become so amazing. He worked hard on his home-schooling and online learning, he did all the jobs around the house, he helped me with the cooking, and we became the best team. There was never any kind of attitude or any resistance when I had to be the parent – which wasn't often. It was like he was happy no matter what time of night it was or what was going on. His smile was fixed and permanent from the moment he went out to get Gi on the porch to the moment he fell asleep. Yes, our family wasn't normal, our lives weren't normal; we lived our lives around an owl for goodness sake. But it worked and we were happy. Nothing and no one was going to ruin that. We had a routine, I made sure that Benjy learned something new every day and that he understood between right and wrong, we kept the house nice – we had even worked out how to keep the exterior nice without being spotted – so we still lived our lives to the fullest. Just in the dark. But that was fine. Wasn't it?

Samuel Collins

The Next Night

The boys repeatedly made fun of me for what seemed like hours in that tent, but I knew that they were secretly hoping for the outcome I was. However, time passed by and there was no sound, no strange noises, and no movement from the empty house. Nothing. It wasn't long before we lost Noah to his dreams, which I can't say I am surprised. The others were losing faith in me too, they had been talking about football for ages now; going from who the best player was, who they would have at their dinner party, who would win in a fight, why they chose to sub people in their fantasy football teams. Their minds had completely forgot about the real plans for the evening, but mine hadn't, I had kept one eye on that house the whole night and I wasn't about to stop now. Even as they're voices lowered, as I could tell they were drifting off one by one, there was no way I was sleeping tonight. I needed to see it for myself, even if they didn't believe me in the morning again.

After I lost all of these useless friends of mine, I decided that it would probably be best to sit outside the tent, that way I would make less noise and would be ready when the time came. I waited for that long that I didn't even quite believe it myself when I saw the shadow of a small boy on the back porch of the empty house. With a short breath, I rubbed my eyes and glared into the darkness. Yes, it was a boy! Surely, he couldn't have been any younger than me. But he was small, and his clothes were even smaller, they didn't even fit him. He looked as pale as a ghost and his eyes were beady and staring into the nothingness of the forest behind our gardens. I do have a neighbour! I knew it. Before I realised, I shuffled onto my knees to get a better view and the crisp grass crunched beneath me. The boy jumped. I jumped. And with that, he disappeared.

Did he see me? Did I see him? Am I going delirious because I've wanted to see something for so long? A boy of my age living next to me then surely I would know, I would recognise him from football; I would see him on the street. Does he live there alone? Why is he up at night? Questions flooded my brain like a tsunami, and I couldn't answer any of them. The boys in the morning will. The more I thought about that the more ludicrous it sounded, the boys won't believe me again, and I don't have enough evidence or answers. They are just going to laugh and tell me it's a dream. I need more evidence, more time. I need to meet this boy.

The next day I chose not to say anything to the boys in fear of the teasing that would retaliate. Instead, I decided that I will repeat the night before, this time with more of an idea what to expect, and therefore more of a plan. So as the night curtains of the sky opened, the darkness encased the street and the boys chatted about nothing important in their tent, it was the first time I realised I wanted the boys to sleep. I didn't offer much to the conversation, because I simply had too many conversations going on in my head. The boys called me weird and boring, but I didn't care. Soon they fell asleep. This was it. Unlike last night, I decided to stay inside the tent. I couldn't risk being seen because I didn't want the boy to retreat into the black hole of his house again. This time, I stayed inside the tent, but I opened the zip so carefully, so that it was only wide enough for the freckles on my nose to freeze and disappear, and one eye that could be fixed on the opposite porch for the duration of the night. Not comfortable, but this seemed like the perfect disguise. I watched and I watched – barely able to even blink. After what seemed like forever the shadow reappeared. This really was it.

Ben

A Million Thoughts

It was almost time to go out to collect my mum. I have been a little nervous tonight; I didn't sleep much, and I know yesterday I was off with everyone, so I needed to make sure I hid my nerves tonight. Last night, I went onto the back porch – like always- and I was hit with a terrifying sight – a boy was staring at me, at us. It was surreal, it's been a while since I have seen anyone that wasn't my dad, but the worst part is... I know he saw me with my mum, perched on my shoulder, almost doubling my height.

I remember going out after hearing the call, and then as I turned, I heard a noise in the distance. Just a quiet noise, last time it was a hedgehog and my dread filled with giggles so that's what I was expecting last night. But no, last night was different – I had a moment where a boy was looking at me – ME. I don't think anyone else was there, and I didn't think Mum noticed from my arm, so I didn't mention it when I got in the house.

But I did sneak a peek from the pitch black of the upstairs window and the boy still stood there staring at the porch. His hair was tatty, and his green pyjamas covered in footballs were muddy – but his eyes remained fixed. There was no doubt that he saw me now. But what would this mean? What is going to happen? Should I have told my dad straight away?

Dad has been strange lately, and it's only been the last couple of weeks since he's got back to his normal silly self. If I was to tell him, he may go back to that bag of nerves again and I don't want that. No, I can't tell him. The boy may think that he had a dream – I just needed to be really careful from now on and it will not happen again.

But here I am, waiting for Mum's signal through a tiny slither in the curtain and I can feel a bead of sweat trickle down my arched spine. It was vital that no one saw me, but I have always wondered why my mum can screech so loud and no one hear. What if they do now? What if there are hundreds of people hidden in that garden next door, waiting to pounce on us. My mother was a force to be reckoned with, she was true beauty and very rare, her feathers glistened in a mesmerising way almost reflecting stars back at you, her eyes told never ending stories, – people would want her. But she's mine and she needs to stay with us.

I scoured the garden next to ours, strategically positioning the curtains so that there was never more than a centimetre gap. The tent was there, a blue oval protruding from the grass that seems to stay there for months on end. I can only guess that this is where the boy was meant to be last night. But I couldn't see any sign of life in the garden.

As I searched the garden as if my eyes had scanner beams, a deafening screech that filled me with joy made me jump more than normal – it was time. Now, normally at this point I dash outside to receive that first moment with mum, she stares at me with those big black eyes and leans her head on mine in silence. Just for a moment, it's just me and her – it's my favourite part of every night. But tonight, that was just too risky. I didn't dash out; I waited by the curtain, scanning the garden for any sign of shuffling, any movement at all. I know Mum will be in view for the garden now, and so if there was going to be anyone it would be at first sight of seeing the gigantic wings of my mother soar down so elegantly. Nothing. I was safe.

I could hear my dad clomping down the stairs, he always spends time cleaning before the arrival of mother and so he wouldn't have noticed my shifty behaviour tonight. He looked at me with confusion when he realised I was in the room with him, when I should be outside retrieving our guest for the night. I refused to acknowledge that this was strange or anything out of the ordinary and I trotted with all the glee I could muster to the back door. I was slow to open in, clearly trying to avoid any creaks or floorboard movement. I allowed the door to sit on my bum as it closed without a sound. I did it; it was shut without a murmur.

As I let out a sigh of relief and looked in front of me for the first time the owl before me had creaked its neck and found a starting position as if to say 'what on earth are you doing Benjy?' I giggled at the thought of knowing what my mum was thinking even when she couldn't say it. Her eyes told her words clear enough – and I loved that.

Although this moment distracted me slightly from the task at hand, I knew I needed to get to her and get back into the house without being seen. This was a mission and I was prepared. I ushered her over to me from against the wall, but she merely creaked her neck the other way and purred at me in confusion. Plan B... I sat on the floor against the door and patted my leg for her to join me. She continued her confusion expression without a blink. Plan C – I was going to have to go get her. I hoped that it wouldn't come to this; I edged out slowly, crossing my gaze from her to the next garden and back like I was watching a tennis match. With each baby step I took I could feel myself panting, I could feel my mums glare and I could feel my gut telling me no.

I got to her, finally. I leant my head on hers and gasped, I realised that this was the sign of relief that there was still no one in the opposing garden… I took this time to tilt my head and take a good look at the old tent that had caused me so much anxiety for twenty-four hours. It was almost like a croissant, electric blue and had rolled down windows. There were a pair of parallel zips at the front, which I presume becomes the door, and they were dark and straight – no not quite straight one had a gape in it. I looked closer trying to make out in the distance whether it was mud or whether it was a hole. Then the gape blinked at me.

Without hesitation, I ushered Mum up onto my forearm and ran for my back door. This wasn't a good idea because the weight of my mum was overwhelming and we both know I can't carry her like that. I have to use my shoulder. She squawked and opened her widespread wings to flutter and stop herself from falling but I buckled under the weight and hit the ground. She continued to flap her wings and hover above me, almost as if she was shouting at my silliness like she used to do when I would push the trolley too fast in the supermarket. She looked at me, but the confused eyes were still prominent. In all the commotion of the fall I hadn't heard the tent zip open; I hadn't heard the grass crunch as the neighbour ran towards my fence. I had even missed the scramble he took to climb over it. But as my mum used her claws to pull me up to a sitting position, the boy's face was right in front of me as he sat on the edge of my porch with his mouth gaping and no words filling the gap. The confused eyes were prominent on his face, too.

Samuel Collins

The Meeting

The moment I saw my chance I took it, *I had* been right, *I had* watched a boy emerge, *I had* watch him see me, *I had* watched him take a tumble when he saw me and *I had* ran and jumped the fence to finally prove my point.

I don't know why I did this, because although it was all I thought about for the last twenty-four hours I hadn't quite made any plans for what to do after I seen him. I ran over but I think I may have left my voice in the tent. It was a slapdash decision, but I knew when he fell it meant he wouldn't disappear into the blackness of the abandoned house, so it was my only chance.

The boy was staring at me and I was staring back. We both had a look of horror/shock on our faces only I wasn't the old with a four-foot beast sitting off on my shoulder – so I don't know what his look was about. I opened my mouth, but the words still hadn't found me. He opened his similarly, but then I noticed the glisten on his cheek as a tear slowly walked down his pale face and there was fear in his eyes. The owl fluttered its wings as if to get my attention and as I moved from one set of staring eyes to the other, I couldn't help but notice the resemblance. They mirrored each other. The owl's eyes were beaming, they were almost hollow, enchanting and they were dark just like the boy.

I felt a sense of calm from the animal, I wasn't afraid. I returned to the boy who was now holding back soft sobs. "I'm sorry," I started. I know I wanted to finally meet this invisible person, but I didn't want to make him cry. "I just, I thought I saw you the other day, and then no one believed me and so I needed to make sure you were real, and it wasn't my imagination." My words had found me in an overload and my explanation had turned into word vomit, the silence was allowing it to keep flowing. "I mean, I thought I saw someone a few months ago and the twins were like yeah, yeah and then it all went quiet. But then now you are here, and you are real, and you can meet them and show them that I'm not craz—"

"NO!" The boy shouted, interrupting the word vomit which I was quite thankful for because I realised, I had forgotten to breathe. "You haven't saw me."

Now I was more confused than ever, "What?"

"I'm begging you, go back to your blue croissant and go to sleep. Please don't come back. You'll ruin my life. You need to go, and you need to not tell anyone."

"What's going on? Are you in danger? Do you need the police?" Thoughts were running round my head more than ever. Why was this boy so scared? Why were his clothes so small, why was he crying?

"No. Please go. I need to go in now I've been too long outside. Please just don't tell anyone."

I looked at him and saw the pain like fire in his eyes. I had to find out more but now wasn't the time.

"Ok. Fine. I'll go... but I'll be back tomorrow."

Ben

Doomed

I walked back into the house wiping my sweat and my tears simultaneously. The last three minutes were a complete whirlwind.

"Benjy, what on earth?!?" My dad came rushing over and immediately knelt before me. I hadn't realised that I had a rip in my tracksuit bottoms and my knee was bleeding. It must have been from the fall.

My dad rushed to the kitchen and came back with his trusty green briefcase. He looked up at me and wiped my tears before attending to my holey knee.

"We need to work on your muscles, young man! Did you hold her how I taught you so you can balance out the weight? Or did you trip on the decking? I'm sorry; I should have replaced it by now!" My dad is so caring and so kind – how could I tell him our world; our bubble has been popped. I highly doubt that the boy is going to keep a crazy, invisible family that includes a giant owl a secret. We would have people knocking as soon as the sun tells us its bedtime. It was over; it was over because of me.

After my knee was patched up, I spent the night feeling the ends of her feathers, watching them catch a glimpse of the moonlight and beam with excitement. They knew, she knew, but she remained calm and normal, so I tried my best to do the same. Dad was jabbering on about his latest painting, occasionally flicking the odd speck of acrylic paint into the air without care for his surroundings. He had grown fond of painting since we became nocturnal. It seemed like a therapy to him, he said it was a nice hobby to have, but I just think it gave him a good reason to sit and stare at Mum for hours on end – even in her new form Dad looked at her with all the love in his eyes that could possibly exist. So, he painted her, in many ways, many styles. He experimented with colours, focussed on specific aspects or sometimes drew her just as she was, perched on the arm of the chair while I ruffled her tummy feathers and smiled at her hypnotising eyes. He was happy while he painted, he was happy when she was there, and so was I.

I couldn't help but continue to feel the pangs of anxiety in the pit of my stomach. I knew I was being quiet and that was making me more nervous. I could see my dad's shifty eyes on me but not daring to ask too much as we aren't great with discussing emotion still. I counted down the hours with each second, anticipating a commotion at our door but nothing came. I waited and waited, wincing at floorboards and gaining a gigantic headache trying to listen to the distant road. Nothing.

I knew that if I was the person who had found a little scruffy boy carrying an owl into an abandoned house, I wouldn't just let it go. I wouldn't just be able to accept that as normal because I've been doing it for years and I still think about how abnormal my normality is. I would be telling people, telling my family and I would be knocking on the door. So why has there been no repercussions to the boy seeing me?

As my mind raced my body found itself drifting into a deep sleep, even before I had the chance to watch my mum soar back to her spiky silhouette of the deep forest.

I woke to the sound of my dad calling me. This was it. They

were here to take him or me or my mum away. I bounded down the stairs trying to explain but getting myself into a splutter.

"Whoa, Benjy, what's up? You've slept in, mate, but that's okay you looked shattered last night. It's nearly time to get our favourite, that's all." I breathed another sigh of relief – this was happening too often lately.

I decided to go out early and sit on the porch for a while, but as I walked out and sat with my legs crossed, the familiar head from the night before popped from the edge of my porch.

"Don't panic," he whispered, in a voice so quiet I could barely hear him. "I just want to talk to you," his voice was calm, and his manner was warm. I decided to stay where I was, he hadn't told anyone so far so I decided I should give him a chance.

Samuel Collins

My Friend Ben

At first it was tiring, staying up to see him, but there was
something about him that intrigued me too much to leave him
and sleep. I decided to keep Ben a secret for now. I went there
and sat speaking to him, I had found the perfect place to sit where
no one inside the not-so-abandoned house could see me, but also
meant that Ben could sit straight ahead and not be seen talking.
He was adamant that the people inside couldn't know that this
was going on. We were only talking, but Ben seemed firm on this
and given his crazy lifestyle, I had to agree with this rule. He told
me all about his life. A lot of it didn't make sense, but I chose to
believe him because it felt like this was the first time that he could
share what was going on. He told me his mum can only see him
at night, and so he and his dad chose to sleep in the day so they
could see his mum in the night. He said that the owl that shows
up also likes to see his mum – but it tended to go a little bit
muffled and shy when I brought up the owl. We talked about
football, and we talked about what I do in school, it turns out Ben
is my age but he is just small, probably because he doesn't get
out much. I offered to get him some bigger clothes, but he refused
because he said his dad would know. He could never spend too
long with me because he didn't want his mum or dad growing
suspicious of his time outdoors. But I didn't mind, I was quite
tired whenever I stayed up with him and I enjoyed our chats, no

matter how short they became.

I felt sorry for him, his life was so restricted; no football, no friends, no Xbox – he didn't even know that there was a new one out. He was a nice lad, someone that would fit well with my little gang on the street. Every time I asked Ben if I could bring them he grew shy and stand-offish, he wanted my friendship because it was forced upon him. But he seemed scared to let anyone else in. Reluctantly, I agreed to keep his secrets and we grew really close in the few weeks that went by.

It turns out that Ben doesn't know much about science, which is my favourite in school after PE, he didn't know much about anything I do in school really. It began to play on my mind while I sat bored in class. I hated school don't get me wrong, but I understand that it's important to know things, and Ben just doesn't. When will he start to go back to normal? How will he get a job? Is this going to last forever? That night I decided to bring it up again, I talked about how school is always talking about 'the future', and I made up some lie about having to write an essay on the qualifications I need for my dream job. I told him it's a lot, and I waited for him to provide some input into the conversation, as so far he was mute.

"Well, I don't need to think about that." He shook his shoulders and tilted his head towards his house.

"Well, this isn't a forever is it? Sleeping every day and living life in the dark?" I asked quietly and trying to sound as friendly as I could.

"Yes it is. This is my forever. Why would I want to change it? I get everything I have ever wanted like this." He retorted and his tone was showing his annoyance at my question.

"What about school, Ben?" I hedged my bet that I had pushed too far, and I was right.

"I'm going in. Night." Ben was already at his back door by the time he had finished his sentence. I retreated back to my own house and stared back at my neighbours before I decided to go in.

I felt an enormous responsibility with these secrets I'm keeping for Ben. But in my head, I don't think it is good for him. Does he realise he's wasting his life in the dark? Should I do something to stop it? Are his parents crazy for allowing him to stay up to see his mum? And I have never seen anyone even go into that house, just Ben and that strange bird of his.

Mr Hooter

Change

My paintings are becoming clearer, my happiness is at a high and my anxiety has improved so much with each day of no drama and no silly boys trying to catch a glimpse of us. The family unit is getting by and it's just how I like it. Benjamin is growing up fast, he has started realising that me and Gi need some time on our own, just to sit and be together. He has started watching the sky at night. After he brings Gi in, he goes back outside, just for a little while and gives us some space – he says that it's nice in the fresh summer air to watch the stars float by. But I know what he's doing; he's giving me some time. He really is growing into a hell of a man.

I watched him one night, through the curtains and he was sat with his legs dangling in the porch, that scruffy hair blowing in the breeze. Even from behind I could tell he was smiling as he looked up at the sky. This is the happiest he has been, I think he is getting used to the routine so much so that he's confident he can spend half an hour away from us and everything will still be fine. It's important he gets some fresh air in his lungs; god knows how small he is for his age. So, I decided I won't comment or ask questions about his time out there, as long as he is happy – I am too.

I have been looking into what I can do with my paintings, the walls are full in our house now and I am getting better and better. One day, maybe this could be a way to fund our lifestyle. Lots of people seem to buy things online these days – meaning I could never have to meet the people who want to buy them. But the only problem is getting it to them. It could be an option for the future when our money is at a struggle. I just don't think I'm quite there yet, quite ready for the world to see my Gi in her newfound beauty.

For now, we have time, as nothing needs to change.

Samuel Collins

Guilt

Crossing the line with a friend is so confusing, should I feel guilt, or should I feel proud that I have helped him – although he definitely won't see it that way. Leaving my conversations with Ben each night left me wondering about how his life will pan out. How could he ever change and snap out of this ridiculous nocturnal-ness if he isn't told to? He is missing out of school so much; he is so small and practically see-through his skin is that pale. It's only spring and I look like I have been lying on a beach when we sit next to each other. So, I made the decision that I was going to tell, I didn't tell it all. I knew if I asked the right questions and grew suspicion in school, something would come of it. I had found out weeks ago that there used to be a boy called Benjamin Hooter in my class, but he left before I moved here. Which, I thought, added up perfectly – but they then said he left because his mum had died so they moved away. Which then doesn't add up because Ben is always talking about his mum. He goes on about only seeing them in the night. Plus, she is the whole reason they do this *stupid* night-time living thing. Ben has never told me his surname, so I don't know about that, but he also never told me whether it was his mum or his step-mum. That's pretty common these days isn't it, to have a step-mum that you call Mum? So maybe, that's who visits in the night and I have got it right. My Ben is Benjamin Hooter. I suppose if you sleep in the day people probably did think he moved away and once a rumour starts that fits, it's hard to remember to truth. So, I decided to keep digging at school.

One day, I was asked to go to the office to deliver a note and I ceased at the chance. The lady who works there loved a chat and I had just the right amount of cheekiness to get away with pushing for a bit more information than I probably deserved.

"Good morning, Mrs Layson!" I began with a cheery welcome, inviting her for a chat.

"Good morning, Samuel, what have you got for me?" she responded in the same upbeat tone.

"Just a note from our class, I think Simon needs a parent calling over his PE kit," I rolled my eyes as if to say: *Kids these days, eh?* 'and she looked at me with a smirk.

"Mrs Layson, can I ask you something?" I tried to sound nonchalant, but she stopped in her tracks and looked at me to go on.

"You know, if a child stops coming to school, what happens?" Mrs Layson put down the note and leaned over the counter separating us.

"Why Samuel? Is something going on? Why don't you want to come to school?" Her expression grew sympathetic and I could tell she was putting on her school face of *you can talk to me.*

"No! No! Not me!" I paused and thought about how I could play this without getting question marks over my head. "I love it here, miss. I just mean, well." Nothing came to me.

"Samuel, it's a hard year you are having, there's pressure at your age I understand. But you know how this school stands on bullying. If something is happening, Samuel, you need to speak up." Her voice was practically a whisper, I could tell this was her training kicking in. The school is absolutely huge on bullying.

Ever since a little girl in the year before got her hair cut with scissors during an art lesson, the school sees every argument or slightly heated discussion as bullying. Some people play up to it, but I just think it goes too far. This also meant though that I knew she wouldn't drop it after this conversation if I don't tell her the truth.

"No, actually... I heard about a boy who used to go here. Benjamin Hotter or Hooter, I think. Well, I know him. I just didn't know why he doesn't go to school." Mrs Layson looked immediately relieved – no bullying this time!

"Oh, what a lovely boy that one was! Lovely family too, bless them." She continued with her papers as if the interrogation over bullying never happened. "Benjamin did leave quite abruptly after, well they had a hard time you see, but they moved away and we never quite found out where to," she paused as if she was replaying what I had said to her in her mind like a black and white movie. "You said you know him, Samuel?"

"Erm, yes, well he's my neighbour, up over on Petunia Grove." I had said too much. I tried to retreat. "Best get going Mrs Layson!"

"No, hold on Samuel. Do you mean he used to be? That's where they did live, but they packed up and left. I spent weeks trying to track them down, to help them after the poor mother died – god rest her soul. I even drove past every night after work for at least a month and every so often since. They have gone Samuel; you must be confused."

Suddenly it became clear that this wasn't a forgotten about boy. This was a mystery that the school have pondered over. For Mrs Layson to go out of her way like that, I think I have definitely said too much. I didn't want to get Ben in trouble: well I suppose I did want them to know. My mind was now playing games on me, I hadn't gone in with a clear plan, I was only meant to be on the inquisitive/research stage of the plan and all of a sudden, I had skipped to telling the school without even realising it. Actually, not just the school, but the nosiest person in the school and I knew she wasn't going to let it rest.

"Maybe it's a different Ben, Mrs Layson. Maybe I have got it wrong. Thanks for your time but I need to get back to class." I have never wanted to be in that classroom more. I sat through my next few lessons trying to reason what might happen now. But I had no idea what this meant for me or for Ben.

Ben

Betrayal

I don't know why I was awake, but I heard the shuffling of the card on the letterbox and the landing of the post onto our never been used door mat at the front door. I could hear Dad snoring in the adjacent room and so I decided it could hurt to go see what junk mail had arrived.

TO THE PARENT/GUARDIAN OF BENJAMIN HOOTER

A school letter.

My hands were shaking as I bent down to pick it up. I'd seen these before; just after the funeral we kept getting lots of these. Dad said they were letters from school about my absences, but they soon gave up and stopped coming through.

So why has it arrived now? What has changed for them to suddenly feel that they could write to us? My brain searched its corners trying to think of a reason behind this soul destroyer that I held in my hand, when suddenly the answer came to me. Sam.

I hadn't meant to become friends with him, I hadn't meant to tell him our way of life – and I hadn't told him all of it. But it was nice to have someone my age to talk to. He was really funny, and he was a really good listener. I had missed him the last few nights when he hadn't shown up. I thought it was because I had been a bit moody last time we spoke. I thought he would get over it soon. But now, this has come through from school and that's the last thing we spoke about.

He has had weeks to tell people about me and he never did, so why once I have decided to trust him would he betray me like this? If the school know, surely my dad will be in trouble for keeping me off school this long. What if they take him? They can't leave me here because they won't believe that my mum is still here. What if they move me? How will Mum know where to find us?

This was worse than Sam seeing me those weeks ago. This was a letter, an important letter. This wasn't just a case of someone believing a story about an owl from a boy with a great imagination.

I couldn't let Dad see this. Without hesitation, I tip-toed back up the stairs and into my room. Beneath my bed I had a tin that I kept all of my secrets in; it had a small photo of Mum (before she changed bodies), it had a little note she put in my packed lunch once telling me she loved me, and it had one of her favourite ear rings. I remember that day that she lost the first one, it wasn't long after we found out she wasn't well, and she was still in the highest of spirits. My dad was twirling her round in the kitchen and her head was back from laughing so much. I was watching on from the breakfast bar, but I couldn't help but laugh along with her. She was begging my dad to stop through her chuckles and when he finally did, she playfully whipped him with the tea towel and called him silly. It was only about five minutes later when she joined me at the table with her breakfast that I noticed she only had one earring in. My dad searched and searched the floors but it was nowhere, Mum couldn't remember if she had lost it the day before and so said there was no point searching after an hour was up as it mustn't have been in the house. It's surprising how often this memory surfaces in my head. It's the laughing noise I love the most, even just thinking of this day and her laughter bounces from the walls.

The final thing was a small silk scarf that still smelt exactly like her. One by one I took each precious item out of the tin and placed the evil letter at the bottom – hiding it with the scarf and placing my possessions on top.

I couldn't help but think there would be more letters to come – seen as the last time there was one every day for at least two weeks. So, my next task was to work out how I could make sure Dad was snoring every time the postman came. Then, the letters would eventually stop – just like last time.

After I had dealt with the letter, I knew that I had to think of a way to see Sam. He had betrayed me; I fell for his calming smile and I told him things I knew I shouldn't. At the first sight of it he ran and told someone. I could not trust him but I also realised that I needed to get him to stop talking about it, somehow take back whatever he has told and get this stopped in its tracks before it goes too far. Although he is now my enemy, I know I need him close by.

Mr Hooter

Mrs Layson

The drum of a fist on my front door darted me awake. It was a stern loud knock, different from the average salespeople who knock as if they are already trying to be friendly and gain your trust. This meant business, they wanted something, and they weren't happy about it. I forced my body to lay still, but my eyes searched the room looking for answers. I couldn't hear movement, which meant either Benjamin was doing the same as me, or he was still asleep. I prayed for the latter. There it was again. Short, stern and serious.

My body had won the fight and I found myself creeping to the curtains. I stood behind for a moment, allowing my body to meet the demands of my panting breath. Quiet footsteps followed, they were heels and their sounds were getting quieter: who ever she was, she was leaving. I plucked up the courage to sneak a peek. My mind was racing with who it could be, but it wasn't pleasurable when I saw the long purple skirt and the emerald blue ford that used to haunt me years ago. She looked a little older, maybe slightly plumper, but it was definitely her. Mrs Layson.

Mrs Layson was keen to be involved when Gi first got sick, she rang regularly and talked about the importance of routine in Benjamin's life. She told us that his absence was a growing concern and that being in school could create a better support network and give him rest bite from the troubles at home. We fell out numerous times over calling my wife and her illness a trouble. But nevertheless, she persisted. She won a few times and Ben was sent in, kicking and screaming over leaving us and me gritting my teeth as Mrs Layson opened that office door as if she was helping us.

When Gi did leave us, it was her name that was on the bottom of all the school letters, it was her knock at my door and it was her crummy blue ford that drove slow past our house looking for us for weeks. She was persistent and I almost felt like it would never end. Even after a few months I would spot her, not every day, but sometimes. I would hear the slow whistle of a car in first gear hovering around my drive.

It had been years since I had seen her last, yet it felt like deja-vu being stood frozen behind the curtain while she spent a longer time than necessary putting on her seatbelt, adjusting her mirrors, topping up that ghastly lipstick that predominately resided on her front teeth. Why was she here?

Eventually her car pulled away and I noticed a floorboard creak behind me.

"Dad?" It was Benjamin and he was lurking at my door with his head lowered.

"Sorry, Benjamin, just a scare. No problem. A lady was knocking, did you hear? Go back to bed son. Soon it will get dark and be time to get up." But Benjamin continued to stare at the floorboards just in front of his feet. He didn't move, he didn't look up, but I could tell something was up.

"Dad," he repeated, his voice quieter and apprehensive. "Was she from my school?" He hadn't mentioned school in years and he definitely didn't seem shocked when I nodded. "Dad," I felt the hairs stand to attention on my arm as he looked at me with a tear dripping from his face, "I made a big mistake."

Samuel

Discovered

It's always strange seeing teachers out of school. You can't imagine that they have a life passed the school gates, and it's always awkward whether to recognise their existence or practise that looking through into the distance kind of vibe and completely miss the greeting of eyes. This time though, I could hardly deny it. Mrs Layson was practically on my drive as I got home from school that Thursday.

"Samuel! Nice to see you," I smiled an awkward smile, waved an awkward wave and turned onto my drive. "So, it's here where you live is it?" I nodded and pointed to my house as if she couldn't see it behind me. "Strange, you see I have been coming here for the last week or so. You know, popping while in the neighbourhood. This is the first time I have seen you; I have been hoping to run into you, to be honest." This would be a creepy thing to hear, but in actual fact I had seen Mrs Layson twice that week. I had watched her stomp down Ben's path and bang on the door as if she was the police. I had chosen to stay out of it, plus I had been avoiding Ben just as much, so I didn't want him to hear me chatting to her and therefore give it away that this was my fault he was now being stalked.

"Now, did you say it was here you saw young Benjamin Hooter?" This was a targeted question, which completely convicted me if anyone could hear so I had to answer and try to save myself.

"Mrs Layson, I think it's a different Ben." Her quizzical eyes didn't believe me.

"In this house, next to yours? Only it seems empty…" She shot me a look that made my whole body nervous.

"Maybe I was wrong, Mrs Layson." I bowed my head; I knew this was a sign of a liar, but it was instinctive, and I hadn't meant to do it.

"Samuel, why don't I believe you?" She walked a step closer to me and I looked over to the top bedroom of Ben's house to check if he was watching. She followed my gaze and she saw what I did. The curtains flickered.

Click, click, click. Off her noisy heels went faster than her body. Stomp, stomp, stomp. Up the porch steps. Bang, Bang, Bang. Her fist hit the wooden door with such force I thought she was going to break in. "MR HOOTER," she screamed. No noise followed.

Bang, Bang, Bang. "MR HOOTER," The commotion caused even old man Burgundy to walk to the edge of his porch and watch.

"MR HOOTER, I SAW YOU. WE NEED TO TALK—"

"Excuse me! You are disturbing the neighbourhood, what are you doing?" Old Man Burgundy to the rescue, thank god! I was at the end of the path, watching the exchange like a tennis match, my feet grounded as if tree trunks had gnarled around my legs, up my body and were covering my mouth.

"They left years ago, lady. You leave that house alone. You think I wouldn't know if there was anyone in that house!"

By this time Mrs Layson was at the edge of Ben's porch and was leaning over to get to the closest possible point she could to old man Burgundy. Her face was red, and her fists were still balled. "I know what I saw, and I am getting to the bottom of this!" she turned on her heels and walked back to the wooden door that had already taken a good beating from her anger. Bang, bang, bang.

"I'm calling the police!" Mr Burgundy announced and he, too, stomped away.

"What a great idea! So will I!" and with that I found myself being in the way of Mrs Layson's heels as she practically ran through me and reached for her car door.

"Samuel," she turned back and tried to seem poised (although it was far too late for that), "you were telling the truth, weren't you? He's in there isn't he?" She paused as if I was supposed to speak but the invisible tree roots still had me captured and I wasn't saying anything any time soon. "Samuel, I'll have to get social services involved. Please don't repeat to anyone what has happened here today. I'll sort this, don't worry." She returned to her car door and hopped in all flustered. I stayed still and silent until the blue of her car had left the road.

I sprinted for the back garden. I needed to speak to Ben.

Ben

Confession

I told my dad everything. I told him about the first night I met Sam and how it continued to run away with me. I told him how we spoke about almost everything. I told him that the only thing he doesn't know…is that my mum is an owl. As I was pouring out more information than I thought possible my dad's face drained of any colour. I expected anger, but I faced sheer disappointment and worry. This was worse than I had expected. I decided that the more I spoke the less chance he would get of speaking. Without realising I was on a loop, repeating everything over and over, saying practically the same words while my tears engulfed my cheeks. I hadn't realised I was in this, or that my dad had moved, until I felt his chest hit my face and he surrounded me. His energy drained into my energy, which then left us through the floorboards. We didn't move for a while, we didn't speak. I felt his hot breath breeze through the hairs on the top of my head. He sighed one last sigh before kneeling down to me.

"Ben, it will be okay."

That's all I needed to hear, I hadn't realised how much was going on my mind since that first letter, I felt lighter now that he knew. We spent the evening checking our house was tight shut. Checking there was no way, that if this lady came back, she would see us. Mum watched on as Dad tried to approach me about this new 'friend' I had. But I wasn't about speaking to him ever again, never mind speaking about him.

By the time the sun opened its eyes we were definitely ready for bed, we had touched up, fixed, checked our night away and it was exhausting. So, Mum said goodbye and we clambered in bed. I felt more confident than ever that we were safe and I decided to ignore that worried face of my fathers – because it definitely wasn't the first time I had saw it, and it definitely wouldn't be the last.

I must have fallen asleep as soon as my head hit the pillow, because when the banging started, I felt like I had only been asleep for a second. I instinctively sat bolt upright, but then I remembered the plan, we were not to move. I tried to put pressure on my ears to do a better job, as I could hear talking beneath me, in front of the house. It was Sam.

Sam was talking to the woman. The evil woman. He was the enemy. Did he bring her here? I had to see. I tried to sneak to the window; my heart was pounding but my need to see the truth was winning.

BIG MISTAKE.

She saw. She saw. She saw.

I had melted to the floor while I listened to more pounding. But then, I heard a third voice. Oh no, was that my dad. I felt my heart stop as I pulled myself up and headed for the stairs. I had to stop him.

"BENJAMIN!" the whisper came from behind me. He was still in his bed, following the correct procedure of remaining still. Unlike me, who failed on day one. I twisted my body to join him but his hand in the air stopped me dead. Stop moving, Ben.

We listened to an argument between the woman and the neighbour; it wasn't Sam's side, so it had to be Mr Burgundy. I could barely breathe in fear of them hearing my unschooled body move. The conversation lowered and calmed; the mumbling became almost impossible to hear. Mr Burgundy had retreated. Was it over?

Was this the end? My mind was racing, we had done it, we had got away with not being seen, not being found out. If we escaped it today, we could escape it every day. Finally, some hope warmed my blood from the ice that had sunk within it.

"Samuel," clear as day, this evil woman confirmed my truth – Samuel was outside my house. I heard her; Dad heard her. I could tell by the way his eyes darted me a look before his brain could kick in and not blame me.

Then we head her again…

"You were telling the truth, weren't you? He's in there isn't he?"

I stared at Dad. He stared back at me. This time I wasn't sad. This time the betrayal seethed through my skin. I was angry. I knew one thing for certain. They weren't taking my dad.

"I've got to go, Dad."

The look on my dad's face nearly killed me. It was as if I ripped out his soul.

"What on earth are you talking about, Benjamin?"

"Dad, if I'm here, they will know you have kept me here. They will take you. If I go, I can sneak back like Mum does. We can stay the same."

"No, Benjamin!" I heard this response, but I was already bounding own the stairs before he could convince me otherwise. My heart was racing, but my decision felt right. I will go and find where Mum sleeps in the forest, I will sleep with her. At night, I will come back home and we'll stay a three. Mum will stay safe; Dad will stay safe. It doesn't matter where I sleep, Dad will be asleep too: nice and safe in our home. Not in a prison cell, while I am sent god knows where else.

I fled out of the back door, I was running so fast I hadn't noticed Sam come around the corner of my back garden and we practically knocked each other out as we fell to the floor.

"BEN! I'm sorry. I didn't mean to—"

But I was not wasting any time to hear what he had to say. I hurdled up and away before my dad could get to me, and especially before that so-called-friend could catch me. For someone who hasn't run in years, I was pretty quick. Their voices became so distant as soon as I got through some trees. The forest was thick and dense, I could disappear here. I ran in directions they wouldn't think to, so that I couldn't be followed. I didn't stop. And with that, I was gone.

Mr Hooter

Abandoned

My boy left me before I had chance to tell him he was being silly. He darted out faster than I could. I lost my boy. I ran after him; I barely noticed the sun hit me for the first time in years. Or the blur of another boy who was lying in my back garden looking dazed. I saw the forest eat up my child, my world crash around me and I fell into a pool of a person on the floor, riddled in a panic attack that hasn't struck me since Gi came back to us. I failed to keep him safe. I failed. I didn't know I was screaming until that boy that was previously in my garden touched my back in a terrified manner.

"Mr Hooter?"

I couldn't see through my tears, I didn't have the energy to lift my head, but I knew who it was. Sam was Benjamin's new friend, the friend that caused all of this. The friend that had told the school, or the police. The friend who forced my son to run away.

"I'm sorry, Mr Hooter."

Through my own distraught I hadn't noticed that this young man was sobbing too. It took all my energy to stand up, but I did it.

"Mr Hooter, we will find him."

I searched the view in front and behind me, the trunks of the trees blended together, they were so tall and thick that even the sun struggled to find its way through. The longing pain inside my heart ached. I looked back at this boy. He seemed taller than Benjamin, a little rounder, too. His face was wet, and his knees were muddy. The knee of his trousers was ripped, and he was bleeding. He noticed me looking at his leg.

"I'm fine, we ran into each other. Me and Ben. I tried to stop him, but I fell and next thing, he was gone."

I searched his expression for some kind of understanding into what he was saying and why I was talking to him, not my son. He was a kid, I couldn't put my anger into him, nor could I blame him for this catastrophe.

"Let's get you home to sort that knee. Then I will find my son."

I barely listened to the boy as he climbed our way back to the garden. I just replayed and replayed our last conversation in the upstairs of my house. Ben was a smart boy. He wouldn't go far. He said about Gi. That's it! He will be back in the night when Gi is due. I was sure of it. The faith in this gave me some relief and I came back into focus.

"—police."

I caught the ending of the sentence and I didn't like what I heard.

"No!" I announced sharply.

"But… but you have to… he's gone. The forest is miles long. You won't be able to do it on your own, Mr Hooter. It's my fault. I will tell the police it's my entire fault. But we need to find him."

"No!" I repeated with even more anger than previously. I watched the little boys face look concerned.

"He'll be back in a couple of hours."

"But, sir—"

"No. He will be back tonight. Now, you listen to me. You

92

have done enough meddling into my life – into Benjamin's life. It needs to stop; you need to not tell anyone about what has just happened. I promise you that Ben is safe with his mother. You need to go home, fix up that knee and forget about what has happened. Benjamin is safe. Now go."

I ushered him to the gate in the back garden.

"Sir, he went into the forest. He is not with his mother. His mum is in work. I think you are confused."

Now I had had enough. He wasn't to find out anything. I realised that Ben had missed this information out of their nightly chats, and I didn't want to see any crazier than I already did.

"LEAVE." I shot him a look that shown how serious I was, and the boy limped out of my back garden for what I hoped was forever.

Samuel Collins

All My Fault

I couldn't describe what happened that day, I was completely baffled. I had watched my secret friend run into the dangers of the forest, I had watched his dad screaming in pain and loss for his son, only to completely switch his whole body and mind and tell me that Benjamin is safe. It didn't make sense. Nothing made sense.

Benjamin had fled not long after Mrs Layson had cornered me in the open air of my front lawn. So, he heard everything. I had tried to stop him but there was no stopping that speed – he nearly knocked me out and I'm twice his size. It was almost as if he was a criminal running from the scene of a crime. Then, I barely had time to process what had happened to me when I saw Mr Hooter for the first time. I didn't even get a good look at him as his speed almost matched that of his son.

It wasn't until I heard the screaming that I picked myself up from the ground and headed towards the trees. I hated this forest, something about it screamed danger – the blackness of the tree trunks, the vast number of skyscrapers that stood tall like an army ready for the kill. But I mustered up all of my brave bones and wandered in slowly, following the screaming. By the time I met Mr Hooter he had calmed but he was still crying. I hadn't realised the extent of the dangers until his emotion hit me hard in the face. I couldn't help but join him in his tears. I knew it was all my fault;

I had brought this man to his knees. I had put Benjamin in more danger than I could imagine. It was me. .

I waited a few minutes before showing myself to Mr Hooter; I tapped him as gently as I could so as not to startle him. It was then when the most bizarre thing happened to me. His first look was filled with anger and hatred and everything that I deserved. But, as he stared at me, he changed. His facial structure changed his wound-up body language relaxed and his anger disappeared. He even offered to walk me back. He seemed worried almost that I was hurt, and it was like he had forgotten all about Ben in that moment.

He even lied to me, so calmly, but he did. He told me Ben had gone to see his mum. Even after we both watched him run into the woods. Even though he was more hysterical than I have ever seen any grown man be. His mum works in the day. I highly doubt it's in those horror movie woods either.

So why would he lie?

Eventually Mr Hooter got fed up of me, and his face was changing shape again, back into the anger I first witnessed. I realised it was time to leave.

He told me that Ben would be back in the night, and that I can't tell anyone.

I mean, that's the one thing I did wrong that caused all this mess. So, reluctantly, I knew in my head that I wouldn't do it this time. I wouldn't tell them that he's gone missing. I mean, if he was going to be back in the night, he wasn't really missing, was he?

Mr Hooter

Two Days Later

It's been two days now and the only thing giving me solace is that I haven't seen Gi either. They must be together. I have spent my nights looking through the forest, but it seems to be never ending. I am starting to regret every decision I have ever made since we drove home from the hospital. What have I done?

My little boy is in trouble, and whatever I do now I will lose him. The realisation that telling the police is the right thing is coursing through my veins, but as soon as I tell them I will have a lot more questions to answer. I have broken the law in many ways keeping him away from the world and all to myself. The ultimate protection I thought, now I realise I have taken away his rights, his education, his chance at normality. But now, if I tell them, he will lose me too, and then they will move him away from Gi. If I don't tell them and he spends another cold night in this forest, he could be hurt, sick or worse. I have crossed so many boundaries, so many lies that I can't find my way back to reality, to being a good parent or to knowing what's best as a parent.

As the moonlight filled the room, I was reminded me that another day without him had finished and I reached for my flashlight and headed for the back door. My plan was ready, the last few nights I had searched left, I had followed the shadow I remembered my son had made and had no luck. I began to feel that the memory was hazed, a hallucination sending me the wrong way. Tonight, I was going right, I was going the opposite to what I thought, but it's been fifty-six hours and my son could be anywhere.

As I edged my way in, attaching a smaller light to my hat, branches broke beneath my boots. The air was cool, but I didn't feel alone. My heart and my stomach both plummeted to my heels for a split second before I realised that it wasn't the hope I wanted. With a fumble and a flashlight, the boy from next door appeared and my heart started to beat again.

"He's not come back has he, Mr Hooter?" Sam whispered, readying his coat as if he was about to walk with me.

"Sam, that's it isn't it, boy? Sam? I really think you have done enough; you need to go back inside and forget about my son. I will find him and I will bring him back." I was serious and the anger flowed but I was determined not to alarm the boy.

"It's been days Mr Hooter; he might need help. I think if we rang the pol—"

"Benjamin does not need police! He needs me! And that's what he is going to get!" I couldn't help it, this boy had outed us to the school, he had made my son run and now he was going to get me sent away and lose him forever. Sam must have seen the venom in my eyes and so he stayed still as I left him to watch me disappear into the forest, like I had watched my son.

In the days, I hadn't been able to come out and search because there had been non-stop calls from the school, and that stupid lady knocking at the door. Today she had even been joined by an extremely round man with a red clipboard and a serious face. His grey checked suit itched and the buttons of his shirt seemed more stressed than him. But they didn't leave for at least thirty minutes. So, I had to admit defeat and hide in the corner of the bedroom out of view and waiting for nightfall.

I stumbled through the forest, arms in front of me feeling the bark of each and every tree, leaving no stone unturned. I whistled the code that Benjamin made every night, hoping he would hear me and know I'm safe and that he can come out of his hiding place (secretly hoping that Gi would hear me and guide me to our boy). I always knew the forest was deep, but I never realised how intense it is. I never thought I would be marking trees with blue chalk to show I have been in this section and my boy is not there. I wanted so badly to become a heap on the floor, but I needed to stay strong for my family, I needed to find him. I couldn't help but cast my mind back to the conversation earlier that night with Sam. His look as I left him wasn't that of sadness and regret. It was confusion. Confusion is a dangerous thing because it means that he is going to make a choice. Bringing the police into my situation will only make things worse, not only for me but for my son. This young boy won't understand that, or maybe he does, and he also thinks my son deserves better. That is where he is right. I need to find him and quick. My gut was telling me that this boy never went back into his house, never had a glass of milk and never went to bed carefree. My gut was telling me that this neighbour who has ruined my life was about to make it harder. Flashings of lights suddenly became clear in the distance, four, five, six minimum. Then, the barking of dogs rang in my ears and declared that the race to find my son had begun. My gut was right.

Samuel Collins

The Truth

It's six a.m. and the police were still in my living room. My mum is fussing about making everybody tea and my dad is whispering and rubbing his head by the mantelpiece. The worrying look he occasionally shot at me made me feel nervous. I was having to tell my story to another police man. I think Dad was more annoyed he knew nothing of this, even though my story dates back to last Halloween. He didn't know I'd been sneaking out of the garden each night to spend time with a secret neighbour, or that I had planned to break into this house. I knew I was getting in trouble for every part I had played in this, but the worst thing was knowing I've waited nearly three days to speak up and tell the police that there's a small boy lost in a dangerous woods. I knew he could be in trouble, he could be dead, and that is down to me.

Mr Hooter was serious when he went back into the forest the night before, more serious than I have ever seen. He told me not to do anything, but that made me feel like I should. If someone has that much worry and fear in his eyes, he needs help. The police will find Ben in no time, I was sure of it. I know the forest is big, but Ben can't be too far in.

"She's dead?!" I had heard the last trickle of a conversation between my dad and the moustached policeman at the other side of the living room.

"She's not. Ben talks about her all the time. He sees her all the time?" Now I was confused, I knew all about Ben's mum. It was practically the only thing that Ben talked about.

The moustached police man edged towards me, he was tall and thin but his shoulders were prominent and made him seem important. He bent down and met my eyes with his.

"Samuel, this is what we are finding confusing. Benjamin's mother passed away a few years ago, she was extremely ill for an awfully long time." I shook my head in disbelief.

"No. That doesn't make sense!"

"None of this makes sense, Samuel. The information you have given us has been extremely useful, and I want you to think about anything you may have missed that he has told you that could be important to the investigation. Our men have been out in the forest for almost five hours and there is no sign of a boy. We essentially are looking for a boy who no one has seen for years—"

"I have!" I was close to crying now, are they going to stop the search?

"How can you not believe me; he ran in there three days ago. His name is Benjamin Hooter. The schools know him too; they have been knocking on the door trying to get hold of him too. His dad was there too! His dad only went in there last night, you must have found him by now; you weren't far behind. Your men aren't looking properly!"

"Samuel!" My dad was suddenly by my side. "The police are doing everything they can Samuel, don't you dare be rude to the inspector!"

"I think you need to go upstairs and get some rest." My mum was calm and collected – a lot more than Dad. She ushered me to the stairs away from the testosterone-filled space that my living room had become. "It's been a long night, love. I understand you are upset. Arguing with your dad isn't going to help now though is it? The police are doing their best."

"What will happen to Ben and his dad? Will they be in trouble?" In all my hastiness to tell the police I hadn't thought about the outcome.

"Let's just get them back safely first," Mum had a worried look in her eyes and I felt it.

They might not come back.

POLICE STATEMENT

In the early hours of this morning police were called to the small estate of Petunia Grove. It is believed that a young boy, aged thirteen, has gone missing in the Royal Oak Nature Reserve Forest at the back of these properties. He has not been seen for seventy-two hours. Full police teams with dogs are now scouring the area in the hopes to return the boy safely. If you live in the area, have had any sightings or know information please contact the police immediately on 101.

TV NEWS REPORT

Next up, we have a serious yet very peculiar missing child case. The police have been searching the Royal Oak Nature Reserve for the last six hours. They have over twenty people on the search, with a team of highly trained sniffer dogs. Now this is a dreadful story as we can't imagine how that thirteen-year-old boy is feeling, but what is peculiar is that we do not have any information on who this boy is. We do not have any photographs, any family stepping forward or a confirmed identity. As you can imagine social media are suspecting that this is actually a big waste of valuable police time and should be stopped. The police are asking if anyone at all could come forward with an information.

The police were phoned initially by another young teen, whose name we cannot mention due to his age. It is said that he lives on Petunia Grove along with the missing child. But it is believed that only he knew of this neighbour. Reports say that there had been no one to confirm what this young man is saying. every person on the street thought that the house was derelict. So, we have opened a poll – Do we think the word of a fourteen year old boy is true and keep searching? Do we stop the search and potentially let a child stay lost in the unforgiving woods forever? Have your say by letting involved in our social media using the hashtag #RoyalOakMissingChild. It is on the screen for you below.

Mr Hooter

Reality

I never made it back to my house that morning. I knew the police would be everywhere. The thought of them being ten steps behind me spurred on my aching legs to find my son. I could not stop. Not now. Three days with no food, no water. Now I'm fearing for his life. Now I am realising the extent of my mistakes. My poor boy has been dragged into this new lifestyle. He didn't deserve this. He deserves normality. And now he could be dead.

My sanity left me when Gi did. The real Gi, whether the owl is Gi or not, I had no right to take away my own son's education, his livelihood, his life. I had no right to be as selfish as I was. I'm paying the price. I will never forgive myself if I don't find him. I felt the cold moss and dew of the bark through my t-shirt as I lent up against an old oak tree, catching my breath and allowing myself to have a minute that I knew I didn't deserve. I had cuts and scratches all over me as I had to turn off my lights when I saw the police. I had to become invisible. This was when I realised how scared my Benjamin would have been without any light, without any idea of where he was going and without anyone to help. I rummaged my way through the leaves, the trees, and the never ending roots that tripped me up with every few steps I took. I was bruised, exhausted and dehydrated, but my determination was still on fire, even though my body was failing to be in tune with it. I pulled out the last of my tissues from my back pocket and swiped my brow, along with the tears that I didn't know I had. I let the sobs fall out of me, just for a few seconds. As I raised my head and let my eyes come back into focus, I noticed a broken branch low down on a big thick trunk of a tree in the distance. It was beckoning me. It pulled me up out of my slump on the floor and towards it and as I moved, almost floating above the debris the floor was built with I heard a grumble.

I was locked in, my palms were sweating, my eyes were transfixed. My aching legs suddenly found the energy to jog... run... sprint. I stopped before the trunk. It was the biggest tree trunk I had seen. It must be hundreds of years old and the gnarls in the tree looked like scars from the past. I took a deep breath. I needed to set myself an expectation so as not to be devastated all over again. But then I saw it, four beautiful, tiny, adorable fingertips grasp the trunk right in front of me. I dropped to the ground as I walked round and saw my boy. There he was. He was huddled into a ball, barely moving and he looked smaller than I ever remembered him. My tears ran away with me as I launched myself over him and tried to get him warm. He didn't say anything, but a tear dropped down his right cheek. I picked him up and pulled him onto my knee. He was barely awake, but he was alive. I rocked him back and forth, mustering with everything I had to make sure he felt safe. Repeating over and over to him that everything was going to be okay. He fell asleep in my arms just the way he did that first night we came home from the hospital. Suddenly we were in my old red armchair again, rocking, sobbing, sleeping, lost in a way that was exactly the same as that night.

I realised that I did need the police, I needed anyone to help me save my boy. I have spent the last few hours running from them in a bid to save my boy from losing me. But now I have seen the truth. We both need saving from our grief. We both need support. But most importantly, my boy needs help right now.

I began to scream as loud as I could and spin my flashlight to attract attention.

NEWS FLASH

In the eighty-third hour of being lost, the missing boy from Petunia Grove has now been found with his father in the southwest of the forest, almost eighteen miles from the street he was last seen in. They both have been air-helicoptered to the Huntington hospital to be treated.

More details to follow.

Ben

Hello

I know you haven't heard from me for a while. But I'm okay.

I knew I had done the wrong thing as soon as I couldn't find my way back, but at the time running seemed like the only option. It was hard, everywhere looks the same and I think by walking to find my way back I ended up further than I had ever been.

The nights were cold and dark, very dark but that wasn't what scared me. I don't mind the dark, my life is in the dark all of the time, I actually like it when it's dark. But what I didn't like was that Mum didn't find me. Mum didn't come to my rescue at the sound of my whistle. It reminded me of the doubt I had when I watched my dad's eyes widen, searching the skies that first night she came to us. That doubt that I had buried in the pit of my stomach.

During the days, as I wandered through the never ending maze, I thought about my family, how much has changed, whether Mum was really Mum or whether we had just hoped it was.

'Losing someone is the hardest thing in the world, people react differently, give him time, Mr Hooter.'

This memory of the nurse talking about me if I wasn't there ringing in my ears the whole time I was in the forest. Did Dad make it up and I just so desperately want to believe him? Was it all in our imaginations to avoid the horror of the loss we felt? Or was my life more magical than anything you can read about?

Despite not having any one or any idea where I was, realising that my owl-mum may not find me, or may not ever again, I still wasn't too scared. Something within me was telling me that I will be fine. As exhausted as I was, I huddled into old giant trees for comfort, something about their energy was soothing, their thick roots surrounded me just like Dad does and I felt warmth within my chest. I slept.

I grew up in that forest – not in a sense of actual years because it was three days – but if you have a magical owl for a mum you would expect her to show up at a crisis like this in the woods. She was nowhere. She was an owl. An owl filled with hopes, stuffed in by both me and Dad.

Dad.

Dad's okay too. He explained everything to the police, well, apart from the whole owl-mum thing. That would definitely get him sent away. He told them that when we lost mum we couldn't cope in the real world with the grief and the loss we felt. He told them he kept up my home-schooling, we were well fed, we had everything – bar daytime and vitamin D. The social services have been in and out the hospital too, but I think they are happy that we are okay. They said they have been to the house and everything looks normal, but that they would be visiting every week until they are sure. We also need to go to counselling twice a week. But to be honest I don't think that's a bad thing for both of us. However, the biggest thing is that I need to go back to school.

Sam from next door has visited too. He came on the first day I arrived at the hospital, therefore I don't remember much of the visit at all. But he did leave me a card. It wasn't like the others – it was an 'I'm Sorry' card. Although he **was** to blame for all of this, I think I'll forgive him. I think it was necessary – but don't tell Dad. I'm actually looking forward to going to school, I'll have a story you know, I won't be a loser anymore. I'm interesting – plus I have a friend now. Sam will look after me, won't he? He has loads of friends, so surely, I'll be fine this time.

I still miss my mum of course. But when I was alone in the forest searching for her in the sky, I felt warmth in my heart. I didn't realise at first what that warmth inside me was. It kept me alive. It kept me safe. It helped my dad find me in the hollow of those tree roots. When he joined me, I felt that warmth spread to him too. It connected us both just how we joined on the big armchair at the fire.

Somehow, that warmth is what told me that I was going to be okay, and that Dad was going to be too.

That was Mum.

Inside me.

She was there all along.

She always will be my warmth inside me.

I still don't know if my mum did become the owl like we thought she did. We haven't seen her since, and I understand now that I don't need to see her in any way but in my heart and my head. She doesn't come in the middle of the night. She is with me always and would want me to live a normal life. Yes, I miss her but I know she is with me, rooting for me, loving me and Dad just as much as she always did.

Grief isn't easy and everyone sees and deals with it differently, but what I can promise is that I will honour and cherish her love more than her loss. I will learn to live and laugh with her warmth.

We will always be a three.